John Fuller was born in 1937 and was educated at St Paul's and New College, Oxford. For the last seventeen years he has been a Fellow of Magdalen College, Oxford. He has published eight books of poetry, most recently *Waiting for the Music* (1982) and *The Beautiful Inventions* (1983). In 1974 he won the Geoffrey Faber Memorial Prize, and in 1980 the Southern Arts Literature Award. He is married, with three daughters, and divides his time between Oxford and his cottage in North Wales. *Flying to Nowhere* is his first work of adult fiction.

John Fuller

FLYING TO NOWHERE
A TALE

PENGUIN BOOKS

Penguin Books Ltd, Harmondsworth, Middlesex, England
Penguin Books, 40 West 23rd Street, New York, New York 10010, U.S.A.
Penguin Books Australia Ltd, Ringwood, Victoria, Australia
Penguin Books Canada Ltd, 2801 John Street, Markham, Ontario, Canada L3R 1B4
Penguin Books (N.Z.) Ltd, 182–190 Wairau Road, Auckland 10, New Zealand

First published by The Salamander Press 1983
Published in Penguin Books 1983

Made and printed in Great Britain by
Richard Clay (The Chaucer Press) Ltd,
Bungay, Suffolk
Set in Poliphilus

Animula vagula blandula,
hospes comesque corporis,
quae nunc abibis in loca
pallidula rigida nudula,
nec ut soles dabis iocos!

P. Aelius Hadrianus.

I

The three novices walked fast down the margin of the hay field. In the great heat the tall grasses stood feathery and still, until the striding sandalled feet parted and crushed them. The hems of the woollen robes caught the seed tips and dragged them. Stems bowed and sprang, sending out tiny clouds of grass fruit.

The garments of meditation are not designed for the pace of prologue; they walked swiftly, though without urgency. At each step their garments were caught between their legs, tugging and chafing their calves. The robed arms were folded, as if to imply ceremony in some decisive preamble.

The girls in the field did not look up from their scything as the novices passed them, but bent more attentively to their work. Their blades swept rhythmically at the base of the standing grass, pulling back the fallen swatches. They moved together against the silent fullness of the field, skirts kilted up about their thighs, feet scratched and bleeding from the stubble.

As they strode by, the novices looked at the girls, and the first spoke a half-voiced thought into the stifling privacy of his cowl: 'Their strokes are like the strokes of the knife on used vellum. The erased word serves its turn and is restored like dead grass to the elements. The field is the book of nature to be freshly inscribed by our brother the sun.' These thoughts were themselves, he reflected, worthy of being inscribed in his book, and he resolved to submit them at the first opportunity to the Abbot for his approval.

The novices left the field and the girls paused in their mow-
ing to look after them. Their expressions showed respect and
concern mingled with a fugitive tenderness. One of them
crossed herself and remained leaning on her scythe, gazing at
the dark-robed young men until they had moved out of sight.
The sweat gathered at her brow and cheeks as if some precious
ichor of the spirit were being pressed and sieved through her
burning face, and in her mind was only one scarcely-
formulated idea, half vocative, half meditative, like a remembered charm of doubtful efficacy: 'Sons of Heaven . . .'

Soon the blades resumed their companionable motion,
edging like an army of moons into the frail and toppling
grasses.

The novices crossed a dry stream bed and descended a
small valley that led to the harbour. They lifted their robes to
scramble down stones, moving together at a variable pace to
negotiate the terrain, moving now closer, now further apart,
but always in a recognisable relationship, like a three-pointed
constellation observed over a season. As such, they were
visible from the boat that was approaching the island, a half-
mile still offshore.

'A welcoming committee,' thought Vane, standing with
one foot on the prow, like a clerk who supposes he is required
to be a hero. He raised his flattened palm to his forehead as
captains did in the theatres, and one of the four winded oarsmen laughed and spat. Vane looked back and reprimanded
him. The man merely grinned, and pulled on his heavy oar.

In the centre of the boat a stallion tethered by each foot
strained and lunged. Its neck was glossy with sweat, panic in
its eye. The head reared and tossed.

'Calm the horse, boy,' said Vane. 'We shall soon put into
harbour. Do you see, they have sent the brothers to meet us.

The boy stroked the neck of the frightened horse and spoke words into its ear. But still its confined hooves slithered on the curving planks of the boat, tugging at the ropes that held them, raising splinters.

The oldest oarsman, who was also the owner of the boat, spoke to Vane:

'So you still think you'll land this horse?'

'I've told you,' replied Vane. 'I need the horse to get about the island.'

'That may be,' said the owner, between strokes. 'But you'll never land him.'

The boy, who was holding the muzzle of the horse as it lifted and showed its yellow teeth, looked questioningly at Vane. But Vane turned away to gaze again at the approaching shore and at the novices who could be seen as tiny figures scrambling over the rocks.

'Where is the harbour, then?' he asked, after a while.

'Why, there it is ahead of us,' replied the owner.

Indeed, the novices had stopped among the rocks, and could be seen handling ropes. There didn't seem to be anywhere to beach the boat.

Vane was alarmed.

'That's the harbour?'

'I did tell you,' said the owner, in weary amusement.

'And the way from the harbour?'

'Didn't you see the brothers coming down?'

Vane was silent, fingering the silver cross around his neck as though this reminder of his status could support him in some practical way in such an irritating adversity. It was clear that you could not ride a horse up a rocky and precipitous incline, and getting out of the boat would also, it seemed, involve clambering over rocks.

'Oh Saviour,' murmured the boy. 'What will become of you?'

The first oarsman spat again, and the boat continued to approach the shore.

Some of the haymakers, heavy-breasted and drenched with sweat, had come to see the arrival of the boat. They were curious to see pilgrims, for there had been none for months. Nor were there any pilgrims now, only a priest and a boy and a horse.

The haymakers lined the cliffs, leaning on their forks among the scorched grasses. Far below them the novices had attached ropes to the iron rings on the twin pillars of old wood that served as a jetty. The wooden platform between the pillars was green and rotten and half broken away, and the novices took care to keep back among the rocks.

It was, as the owner of the boat had said more than once, impossible to land the horse. The rowers rested on their oars some yards from the rudimentary jetty while a rope was thrown, and at this the stallion became terrified. The hay-makers could hear the confused shouts of the oarsmen and the whinnying of the stallion as the long boat lurched danger-ously in the rocky inlet.

'Saviour, keep still!' came the boy's cry.

But the horse would not keep still. Its frantic efforts had loosened the rope around one of its feet which now kicked out and sent one of the oarsmen into the water. The others no longer could keep the boat properly aligned. The oars grated on the rocks and looked in danger of snapping.

For a moment, as the stallion strained, it seemed as if it might spring from the boat of its own accord. As the rocking of the boat added to the natural turbulence of the waves, so it seemed that the black beast was itself some manifestation of the sea. The absurd wooden structure of the boat seemed only an encumbrance, both preventing the horse from reaching the shore and from falling back into its element. The creature strove fiercely, muscles and veins starting out from its neck and flanks, arched like an embodied wave, sprung and not falling, but about to fall, as though penned by a draughtsman with a patient eye. The whinnying was pitiful to hear.

'Still, Saviour! Quiet!' commanded the boy.

Even from the cliffs the sound of splintering wood could be heard. The oarsmen now had both ropes from the jetty lashed to the forward rowlocks. The boat was stable and could be slowly drawn into the required position, but the stallion's hooves threatened to stamp through the bottom of it.

'Cut the rest of him loose,' shouted the owner. He signalled to the rear oarsman to cut the ropes that bound the back hooves at the same moment as he freed the front hoof. The oarsman who had fallen overboard was now clinging to the side, hair and beard streaming, nostrils full of blood.

'Are you mad?' cried Vane. 'We shall lose the horse.'

'That, or I'll lose my boat,' said the owner. 'None of us will get back to the mainland then.'

Vane's face was pale with rage.

'There'll be another boat. I'll pay you in full for this one.'

'There's never another boat. No one is fool enough to work the straits but me. No one would risk these currents for an island of lunatics but me.'

Vane was crouched in the prow of the boat with both hands clutched to the sides against its lurching.

'The pilgrims pay you well enough,' he shouted.

'Pilgrims?' laughed the owner. 'I've rowed over no pilgrims since the spring, and rowed none back neither, for twice as long. As well you know, father, for that is why you are here.'

Vane knew the truth of this, and suspected that it was also true about there being no other boat. He certainly did not want to be forced to stay any longer on the island than he could help.

'You'll come for me as we agreed?'

'If I have a boat left to come in. Cut the horse loose!'

Vane and the boy stood by powerless and frustrated as the horse Saviour was cut free. The novices were pulling on the ropes to bring the boat into the jetty, and to the haymakers on the cliff it seemed as though everything was going to plan and that the horse would leap from the boat on to the jetty.

But the distance and height were too great and the state of the narrow planks too precarious. Saviour looked wildly to right and to left and jumped towards the rocks, sending another oar into the water and unbalancing the oarsmen in a heap on the floor of the bobbing boat.

The hooves struggled to keep the body upright, but one leg was already broken from the jump and as the horse heaved, sank and scrambled among the slippery rocks other bones failed him. For a moment it seemed as if the glistening torso would try to move by itself in a series of wriggles and lunges, dragging with it the bunched and useless withers and fetlocks. One rear leg was flattened at an unusual angle from the knee; the other seemed caught between two rocks. The animal's neighing and trumpeting echoed in the bay.

On the cliffs the haymakers wept, and one of them clasped to her shoulder another who could not bear to watch. The first novice, who had been directing the others in the correct way to manage the ropes, stood back from the scene in wonder.

Within the darkness of his cowl he thought: 'The sea-god Proteus, finding himself trapped and surrounded in one of his favourite metamorphoses, struggles in fury to find his former shape.'

With the Abbot's approval, this too might take its place in his book of meditations.

2

'A pity about the horse,' said the Abbot. He lifted and shook a small bell, and gave instructions to the novice who appeared at its call.

'Saviour was given to me by the Bishop himself,' said Vane.

'We have animals here on the island,' said the Abbot. 'You need not go about on foot.'

'Animals?' queried Vane.

'Animals,' repeated the Abbot, decisively but without further specification.

The novice brought in a wooden bowl of milk which was offered to Vane. He took a sip from it and set it down on the table between himself and the Abbot, who was now looking out of the window.

'You will want first to visit the well,' said the latter, without interest.

'I shall indeed want to visit the well,' said Vane. 'But first I must take some depositions on the question of the pilgrims.'

'Of course,' said the Abbot. 'The pilgrims.'

'Are you not yourself concerned about the pilgrims?'

'I would say,' replied the Abbot vaguely, 'that I should

certainly be concerned *with* the pilgrims, were there any, but that I am not much concerned *about* them.'

Vane concealed his irritation.

'Have you any idea why there are no pilgrims?' he asked.

'Ah,' said the Abbot carefully. 'That is a deep question.'

'It is a question I shall have to ask. One of the principal questions. The Bishop is much concerned.'

'The devoted no longer believe so fervently in the efficacy of such cures as we advertise. It is a doubting age.'

'We are not, I hope, to share in such doubt?'

'I explain, but do not prescribe. The journey is difficult, the miracles uncertain. I do not blame the problem on the pilgrims who do not come.'

Vane considered this.

'A pilgrim who does not come is not a pilgrim,' he suggested.

The Abbot shrugged.

'A miracle which does not occur is not a miracle,' he replied. 'And perhaps, for both these reasons, there is no problem.'

'The problem,' said Vane, 'may well be one of the availability of Church funds.'

'Ah,' nodded the Abbot.

'And there is the problem, too,' continued Vane, 'of the pilgrims who have not returned.'

'Why should they return?' inquired the Abbot. 'You know that for many the journey is the final quest of a life committed to worship. The pilgrims' road across the mountains of the peninsula to this island is not an easy one. Many are old. When finally they reach us, as if grasping a hand held out in comfort and alms-giving, they are content to die.'

'I have lists, and testimonies from relatives,' said Vane. I, shall wish to inspect graves.'

'To inspect graves?' murmured the Abbot. 'Of course.'

Again he looked out of the window, almost as if a grave or two might be glimpsed from it. This gesture, and his general demeanour, served as an indication of his wish that his relationship with Vane should reach at an early stage a useful degree of informality. But the interview remained a critical one, nonetheless, and Vane, sipping at his bowl of milk with his eyes fixed on the apparently abstracted Abbot, was put on his guard.

That same evening he retired early to the room which had been put at his disposal and unlocked the chest which contained his papers. Carefully he read over yet again his episcopal warrant, and instructed the boy to cut pens and make fresh ink. Then he prayed for guidance in his undertaking.

3

The Abbot slept badly. His own evening hours were available to novices who wanted to consult him on personal matters, and this lending of an ear and bestowing of advice usually served to distract him from his own thoughts, and to bring sleep. However, on this occasion the preparations for Vane's visitation had already interrupted his daily routine of contemplation and investigation, and the evening visit of the senior novice with new material for his book of meditation prompted still further concern with their guest. From this novice the Abbot was able to gather a full account of the incident at the harbour, with details that Vane himself had not supplied—the loss of a packet from the mainland directed to the Abbot himself; the full degree of discontent of the boat-owner; the insistence by Vane that he be carried up the rocky shore and the calling-down of the sturdiest of the girls from the hayfield to perform the service, and so on. The Abbot was not pleased with any of this, and resolved to watch Vane more carefully than he had thought necessary. He questioned the novice closely, and paid scant attention to the young man's own observations beyond remarking that the book of nature was not to be erased since it had been written for all time and only our ignorance of its future pages hinders our full under-standing of its larger plan. 'That was not what I meant,' thought the novice. 'He has something on his mind. He has not been listening at all.'

When the Abbot blew out his candle at last and settled his head on the pillow his thoughts were of the difficult satis-faction of Vane and of the absence of graves.

He would fall asleep and wake abruptly at the very moment of unconsciousness with a distinct and curious jerking of the left shoulder. He was ready for sleep, he knew, and yielded to it willingly, only to find himself startled and wide-eyed at this involuntary motion of the neck and shoulder.

He lay on his right side, with his right palm under his thigh and his left palm flat down under the pillow, legs bent and crossed. A single sheet of fine linen soon became clammy in the heat and was thrown off. He tried the same position on his left side, was immediately uncomfortable and returned to his right side.

He was unused to visitors with whom he must converse on a footing more equal than that of master and pupil. Had he given to Vane the impression that he was sceptical of miracles, and therefore of the curative power of the Saint's well? Perhaps he had. If so, he regretted it, for though Vane was an intelligent man unlikely to find reason to be committed to the superstitions of the mass, he was here in a critical, investigative, potentially hostile role. Any remark of the Abbot's which might seem at all relevant to his inquiry would certainly be noted in his papers for possible use in his conclusions—unlike his comments to the novice, for example, which might on serious reflection appear more precisely heretical. Who should assert without danger, reflected the Abbot, that natural law was immutable and already written? Didn't that seem necessarily binding upon God who was, after all, the legislator of that law? Was it not, indeed, the rationale of disbelief in all miracles, whereas his conversation with Vane had touched only on the evident unlikelihood of such prevalence of miracles as the existence of shrines required? The Abbot concluded that it probably was, and that it was a good thing that he believed he could rely both on the discretion and, alas, on the essential obtuseness of the novice.

Soon he fell asleep again, but was immediately woken by his strangely jerking shoulder. He knew that he had somehow strained this shoulder, and now remembered how.

In the early hours of that morning he had gone down to his study, using, upon some whim, the second staircase. This staircase was one that he hardly ever used, being a narrow circular one of stone fitted within a buttress of the house. Its steps were worn and their descent precipitous, around a central stone pillar which it was advisable to cling to with the left hand.

Thus he had descended, his mind not so much on his studies as upon how to remove such traces of them as might provoke awkward questions from the official visitor, due that day if the tides permitted. The dissecting chamber was well enough out of the way. He sometimes couldn't find it easily himself in the mazes of the house. And the library he always kept locked, too, out of respect for those silent guardians of words, laboriously accumulated. Whatever lay casually in his study that Vane's eye might light on—a forbidden mono‑ graph, perhaps, or a gland in a little dish, brought from the chamber for longer reflection upon its secret properties—he intended that morning to hide away.

But the rhythm of the stone stairs and the coolness of the central pillar beneath his palm distracted him. The pleasure of leaning at a slight angle above his feet as he placed them one after the other at that precise point on each triangular wedge of step to lend at once enough width for momentary balance and enough narrowness for downward spring and propulsion was combined with the pleasure of the friction within the light grip of his hand and kept him moving on even after he had come to the small wooden door that led to his study.

Perhaps he was still not properly awake. He tried to remember if he had known before that the staircase continued beyond that point. But whether he had known or not did not seem to matter, for it indubitably did. On and on he went, faster and faster. As he descended it became cooler, and although the Abbot's heart raced from the exercise and his shoulders and sides were damp with sweat, he felt about his cheeks the dead cold air of cellars, and the stone beneath his palm was wet.

Round and round he went, now taking two steps at a time. It had become absolutely black so that he could not even see his feet beneath him. He supposed, therefore, that at any moment the stairs might come to an end and that he would be brought up with a jolt. But the continued sense of an unsee‑

able void beneath him and the obsessive movement of his legs carried him on, dizzyingly.

He did not understand how the stairs could continue for so long, or where they might lead. His left shoulder ached, as did the muscles of his shins and the front of his thighs. At times his right shoulder brushed against the circular containing wall of the stairway, and he knew that the descent was narrowing. It was also now less cool and the air less easy to breathe, the pleasant cellary mustiness succeeded by a rank metallic stench. But the stairs went on.

And then there had come into the Abbot's mind a vague image. It was less a mental embodiment of any ascertainable shape than a substantial, though imprecise, formulation of a sudden unwillingness to precipitate himself further down that winding stone flight. He knew that he might put the image from his mind. He knew very well that in his automatic downward motion assisted by gravity and the concentration of darkness, he might ignore the image, refuse to yield to it.

But there was something about the image that compelled him to yield. And he had yielded, succumbing to a sudden terror that brought out the hairs on his neck and beard and rooted him to the stone above the interminable stairway, his head spinning.

On his way up he counted three thousand and eighty-seven steps before he reached his study door.

This was the reason for his strained shoulder and his difficulty in getting to sleep. But curiously enough, having remembered the reason, the Abbot became drowsy again in contemplation of the unending stairs, and this time the troubling alertness of his fatigued muscles found an appropriate object in his own memory: thus he fell asleep dreaming not of the troublesome visitation of Vane but of his descent of the stairs that morning. In the dream it became hot, as though the stones had been lifted from a fire to warm a bed. And in his dream, hot as he was and totally gripped by fear as he passed the three-, the four-, the five-thousandth step, in his willed dream this time the Abbot did not stop.

4

During the following day, Vane covered many sheets of paper in his forthright unhurried hand. Bells rang at the appointed hour for the divine offices, but Vane, who had attended matins after rising, and shaving his finely-sculpted chin as best he could in tepid water, ignored all calls to devotion and kept at his work. At midday he was brought two wooden bowls, one containing ewe's milk with bread crumbled in it and the other boiled plantains. He ate some of this food without enthusiasm, while reading over the accounts he had made of the morning's interviews. Flies buzzed in the pane of the one small window through which the sun streamed between the thick stone walls.

Working in the relative coolness of his room all day, Vane did not suffer from the unusual heat. He noticed, though, that most of the novices who came to answer his questions were exhausted and listless. They spoke briefly and without interest, saying no more than was necessary to respond to his interrogation with a dutiful politeness and the appearance of honesty.

In the afternoon he was visited by the Manciple, a lay brother of unpleasing appearance who said least of all. He had a squat heavy head, with dark eyebrows and patches of unshaven bristle on his jowls. He appeared to have almost no neck and kept his face entirely and fixedly on Vane's, grinning hideously in what appeared to be an equal measure of stupidity and guile. To some questions he simply nodded or assented, when a statement of fact or choice of alternatives had in fact been required of him. At one point he ignored a question altogether and, glancing at the half-eaten bowls over which the flies now crawled in close abandon, asked if there was not some kind of food which Vane particularly craved and which might perhaps be obtained for him? Was he used to meat? They did not have much meat on the island, but every effort would be made to make their distinguished guest comfortable. He had only to give the word.

Vane muttered some reply, put down his pen and warily rubbed his eyes. He felt that he was, in general, getting nowhere. When the Manciple had left, he rose and walked about the room, observing idly the suggestive shapes formed by the cracks and flakes of the whitewashed plaster. Later, after nones, the Abbot returned to make inquiries about his progress, genial but unrelaxed, like the bedside visitor of a sick man.

'You have no register of pilgrims,' complained Vane.

The Abbot raised his eyebrows.

'Should we have such a thing?' he said, in surprise. 'Who is to tell who is a pilgrim and who is not?'

'It would have been advisable,' said Vane.

'And laborious,' replied the Abbot. 'It would require interrogation of boat passengers, a system of classification. We don't have the time for such a thing.'

'Should you not know who is on the island?' asked Vane.

'Visitors to the island hardly go unnoticed,' said the Abbot. 'They need lodging. Either here or at the farm.'

'And those who lodge here are pilgrims?'

'Possibly.'

'They attend at the well to be cured?'

'Possibly.'

'Come,' urged Vane. 'The miracles of Saint Lleuddad's well are the foundation of the abbey's charter. The well is the object of all the pilgrims who follow the long saint's road to the island to be cured.'

'Or to die,' said the Abbot.

Vane sighed.

'We seem to have had this conversation before,' he said.

'Please don't misunderstand me,' said the Abbot. 'Pilgrimage is a symbolic act, is it not? It is only the outward sign of an inward direction. It is the earnest of our spiritual condition, a manifestation of the natural tendency of life to seek its fulfilment. Life is not a condition for which, I think you will admit, there is any cure.'

'I hope you would not say such a thing to the Bishop,' said Vane. 'There have been many bequests for the upkeep of the well, in gratitude for the cures it has effected.'

'Or in the hope of the reward of health,' said the Abbot. 'The Bishop's exchequer is heavy with the remorse of the rich.'

'Heavy enough to support the foundations of this abbey,' put in Vane.

'I acknowledge it,' said the Abbot. 'But I cannot arrange cures. Cures are not for sale.'

'Are you saying that there are no cures?' asked Vane.

'Perhaps there have been cures, but I do not know in every case what has caused them,' replied the Abbot.

'When was there last a cure?'

'I cannot say.'

Vane frowned and was silent. After a moment he went to his papers on the table and looked through them, picking one folded sheet out with deliberation.

'I think I should read you this,' he said. 'It is only one of many pieces of evidence that has reached the Bishop that something is amiss here, but it will serve to represent them all. And I hope that when I have read it to you, you may have some answer to give me.'

The Abbot inclined his head slightly in acknowledgment.

'It is one of a number of letters written to his brother in Chester by one William Evans, an innkeeper of means, a widower. He was afflicted with headaches, spells of dizziness and vomiting that became so severe that he decided to leave the inn in the capable hands of his trustworthy tapster and under his brother's occasional supervision, and to undertake a pilgrimage.'

'Are there no doctors in Chester?' interposed the Abbot.

'Physic could do nothing for him,' said Vane.

'I suspect he needed a change of life,' said the Abbot.

Vane ignored this.

'I shall read the letter,' he said. He read it, and the Abbot listened, looking out of the window.

5

Brother Hugh, I told you of the portent of the eel which I waited for two days and grew rheumy in the waiting what with the closeness of the well and the water blood warm and above the knees not fresh like Pin y Wig the rill in Nefyn parish that cures knuckles and hands clean and cool like new ale from the cellar this being not moving and lying still and hard to see the bottom at the end that is deepest where one of our number though an old man and with a terrible crusty mouth and nose still of good sight and fair understanding and a tolerable companion says he saw shapes as it were oranges under the water or another time like hedgehogs without their prickles which makes me fearful to sit there so long were it not for the portent of the eel which they say is certain if it should wrap itself round your legs in a tight embrace will effect a cure be it of small ills like warts or boils or the being unmarried and not liking it which I did ever think a condition to be more praised than regretted or whether of grievous pain of great lameness, chancres, ulcers, blindness and the like the cure of my head being of this degree of hope and gravity so I sat two days for the eel without luck but it happened that a young girl a simpleton was brought in by her mother and stood there in her shift stooping and stirring the water about with her hands as it were a soup of delicate making and the mother standing by and drinking the waters and talking loudly of all the calamities that had ever befallen her and we sat round the edge of the well not able not to listen but nodding at her to show we did listen the girl gave a great shriek and was lifted out with the eel fast around both legs together like a hoop on a barrel and it could not be prised off by two men within ten minutes and we heard later from the farm that the girl had died of fright so much for the portent of the eel which I now think to be unreliable like the pair of trout in Ffynnon Beris which made their appearance while I was bathing but did in no way lighten my head and I caught a chill moreover from the water which I do believe descended from the mountains with barely melted snow in it though here on the island nothing is cold not even in the night which can be as close as day and in the well is moist so as to bring on a tightness of the chest and difficulty of breathing which greatly affects the oldest among us they being too weak to move elsewhere to cooler places such as the cloisters of the abbey or to the dairy of the farm where indeed better provision may be had as curd cheese freshly made

and a manner of herbs in a pot but no ale for it is not drunk nor made
and they do not kill their beasts for they only ride them or milk them
and I think the beasts become their friends too familiar to kill and too
famous to be missed and I long for a great leg of mutton boiled in broth
for I think you would not know me thin as I am now and ill not only
from the weight and spinning of my head which indeed I am much
resigned to but a looseness of digestion from the diet and the waters and
a strange feeling over all other feelings like a small fever which the
others also complain of and never complained of before though some of
us have been together for many months and suffered together too like
Walter from Anglesey who was robbed at Fynnon Alhaiarn and
Master Hughes who found he could not move his bowels for a week
after he had made a collyrium from his scrapings of the columns of
Saint Beuno's chapel in water of the spring there and drank of it
mightily though I told him it would bring on the stone and they were
truly pagans at Clynnog Fawr and not to be trusted for I was
informed they did offer heifers to Saint Beuno like a god of the old
world and not a Christian saint and I told Master Hughes who would
not believe me but still he is recovered from his costiveness now and
might wish some of it again as all our motions are frequent and watery
and some take it as a sign of the working of the waters for a flux is as it
were a kind of baptismal purging of the inside part of a man which is
the unwholesomest part as I heard the Abbot say in a sermon here who
speaks strangely and for the most part hardly to be understood as for
example the devil is nothing but the world and the flesh which we
consume and therefore accommodate though our spirit cannot bear to
contain him and strains to dispel him and if we were pure spirit would
live only on air like the angels do which Walter from Anglesey
reckoned was a poor argument against roasted mutton however there is
not much hope of debating the Abbot into a host for we are all too weak
and I cannot say that there is much money left between us for none can
but ill spare a sixpence to the boatman for the carriage of a letter and

he bur rarely comes complaining of the tides and the niggardliness of the pilgrims which is as I know a lie for all the pilgrims are overjoyed to reach the island and the shrine of Lleuddad and pay the surly boatman more than he deserves for his little pains so that there are some among us who fear that they may not have enough to return to their homes and hoard their pieces or sew them in their clothes so they may not be tempted to spend them on messes at the farm and instead they fish for eggs that have been cast in the well and eat them with the bent pins that they find which those with warts have bepricked themselves and also cast in the sacred waters for a cure and aggravate their fever with this and similar unwholesomeness which the Abbot has spoken against like the practice of taking the grass that grows about the church wall and eating it between bread for it is reputed to have the pure virtue of the waters uncontaminated by the washing of the sundry limbs and private parts of the pilgrims and this grass they call porfa'r cynddeiriog the grass of the mad and truly they are like so many Nebuchadnezzars that eat it for one such crawled about all night on his fours and moaned like a beast and those that he has awakened talked among themselves and we asked ourselves if we would ever leave the island in good health for it did not seem such a great thing to ask of God who has placed his saints and their acts to guide us and who would not keep us on the island in unhappiness unless for a purpose and what that purpose might be none can tell though the old man with the crusty nose whose name I can never remember took us to see the graves of the pilgrims and their stones were so many pages standing out from the Book of Judgement and all containing every single name that ever was and these the old man claimed were God's saints and it was a great honour to be buried here though Walter from Anglesey said that we had seen none of our number buried who had died in the time we had been there and fell to complaining that the Abbot would require a great offering of gold to secure six feet of the island in perpetuity and that it was no good enquiring of the brothers on any matter whatsoever for they never spoke *but moved about with their monstrous hoods up like dancing bears thinking of their own salvation but of no one else's wherefore I begin to think it is time that I returned to Chester and to the Bell for I am sure your mind is not on selling ale and mine is no longer much on my cure, your devoted brother William.*

6

'Well?' asked the Abbot, when Vane had finished reading. 'What is it that you want to know?'

'There are many questions,' said Vane, 'which arise from the sort of thing referred to here and in the other evidence in my possession. What arrangements do you make to bury the dead?'

'The usual arrangements,' said the Abbot.

'What might happen to those who die and are not buried?' asked Vane.

'If we cannot recover the body of a drowned man,' replied the Abbot, 'then naturally we cannot bury him. No one else who dies here leaves the island. It would be hardly practicable to remove a corpse.'

'I know the journey by boat is hazardous and no doubt is more so in winter months. But are you saying that all who are ill and die on the island are buried in the island cemetery?'

'Those who do not drown, yes.'

'I see. Then William Evans of Chester and Walter Prichard of Anglesey and many others whose names I have here as being reported missing will have found burial places on the island?'

The Abbot shrugged.

'Unless they have now returned home,' he said, 'or have gone elsewhere.'

'You have not been witness to the anxiety of their families and of the priests in their parishes. That is why you can say such a thing,' said Vane.

'Not at all,' replied the Abbot. 'I understand the concern. But as I said before, a pilgrim is by definition one who has begun to make a decision to change his life. To seek change is very often, believe it or not, to achieve it. These good people may very well have gone elsewhere.'

'I cannot believe it,' said Vane. 'William Evans states his intention of returning home.'

'An innkeeper who cannot keep upright?' smiled the Abbot. 'Perhaps you are right and he would soon crawl back to such a liberal and ready supply of liquid oblivion. But I do not find a tipsy man a reliable witness. His remarks about my sermon, for example, reveal an inferior understanding.'

'How?' asked Vane.

'The parable of the Devil as the excrement of the created world is a heresy that I was at pains to illustrate and then confound, for it is the opposite of my belief. William Evans must have succumbed to his dizziness at that moment. My sermon concluded with the assertion that the world is precious beyond our understanding, and that we are a part of it.'

'Indeed?' said Vane, suspecting that it was in fact the Abbot's belief that was heretical. 'It remains part of my duty to investigate your arrangements for the pilgrims' welfare and to ascertain the whereabouts of Evans and others like him.'

Their interview was concluded with Vane's resolve to visit the well and the cemetery on the following day. The Abbot arranged for the provision of an ass and an accompanying novice, but excused himself from the visit on the grounds of the pressure of his duties, and, leaving Vane to the transcription of his interrogation of the novices, retired to his dissecting chamber.

7

The evening sun hung on the shoulder of the mountain and lit up the whole garment of the sea. The island seemed to float in darkness that sought the disappearing light. It was like a still voyage towards the shining edge of the world.

After the bell for compline, the only sounds were the questionings and responses of sheep, ewe answering lamb as they grazed. But now and then came the hoarse rattling of a buzzard taking food to its young. Everywhere was still, except that among the grasses creatures whom the day had shut in with its invisible doors of heat came out blindly and inquisitively. Moths fluttered through air that seemed no thinner than their dusty wings, and even less substantial insects seemed to be suspended in the night warmth, aimless motes apparently designed only to reflect and magnify the smallest glimmer of the lost light.

At the farm the youngest girls had long been in bed, for it was they who had to rise earliest in the morning to do the lightest work. The cleaning was theirs, and the feeding of animals and the baking of bread.

But it was too hot to sleep. They lay unclothed on their beds in the long low loft under the eaves of the farm and made faces at the sloping ceiling.

Sometimes one would talk, sending out words into the darkness that were not like the words of the daytime. The

voice was not conscious that it belonged to anyone, only that
there were ceremonies and speculations of the night to which
everyone unconsciously contributed. There were stories, of all
kinds. And on occasion, one of the girls might rise and run
between the beds, as if to illustrate in half-dance the climax of
a narrative, or simply to punctuate the slow advance of the
night with a gesture, like that of raised arms and rotated wrists,
which might lend it grace.

'Gweno, Gweno,' came a whisper.

There was no answer at first.

'Gweno!'

'What?'

'Tell about the brothers at the pump.'

'No.'

'Go on, why not?'

'I'm dying.'

'Are you dying, Gweno? I'm truly sorry.'

'I'm wrapped up in a leaf very quiet and still. My legs are
together and my arms are at my side, and I'm wrapped in a
leaf and hanging from a tree on a thread, turning very slow.'

'Is it painful, Gweno?'

'No, it's beautiful and there's the breath of the wind turning
me slightly. Can't you feel it?'

'Yes,' said another voice. 'I can feel it.'

'Now the leaf is drying and crackling. It's crumbling away.'

'Are you crumbling away too, Gweno?'

'No, no. It's leaving me pure and new and now I've died
and got wings and I'm flying away. Can't you see?'

Her fingers fluttered in the moonlight, and their shadows
moved in the rafters.

'Yes,' came several voices. 'We can see you flying away.
Where are you flying to?'

'I'm flying to nowhere. I'm just becoming myself.'

There was another silence, a longer one.

Then came another whisper.

'Tetty, tell about the brothers.'

'Tetty's asleep.'

'No, she isn't!'

Tetty was not asleep, but was holding the flowers of her breasts and filling them in her mind like filling cupped hands with the heaviness of spring water, trickling cool through the fingers. She listened to the voices in the dark.

'Tom Barker, Long Rachel, Minnie Wilkin, Milly Larkin and Little Dick were all in the same bed one winter night and the blankets piled high. They had prayed to the Saint and blown out their five candles and they had one apple only to eat between five.'

'Yes, yes! What then?'

'There was a bumping sound on the roof. Like this: bump, bump, bump.'

'What was it?'

'They didn't know what it was. So Tom Barker shouts out quickly: "Who's there?" And a voice comes back: "It's only the wind walking over the roof." "Oh," says Tom Barker. But then came the bumping louder and Long Rachel calls out to it: "What are you, then, bumping up there?" And another voice says: "It's the clouds walking over the roof." "Oh," says Long Rachel.'

'Aren't they frightened?'

'Yes, they're very frightened. Very very very frightened. So they prayed again to the Saint. But then there's more thumping up above, and so Minnie Wilkin says: "Who's that, thumping on the roof?" And a voice says: "Nothing. Only the moon." And they can hear a hissing sound move slowly over them like a great cold fire. Then there's another banging and a clatter and Milly Larkin asks: "What's up? What is it now?" And another voice replies: "It's the stars passing by." "Oh," says Milly Larkin.'

'Are they still frightened?'

'They're still very frightened, and they've all gone down in the bed. Then comes the loudest noise of all, a rumbling and a rolling and a smashing and a crashing all over the roof, and Little Dick whispers from the bottom of the bed: "Who's there?" And a big deep voice replies: "It's the Saint himself passing by, and herding the wind and the clouds and the moon and the stars before him, and all is well." "Oh," says Little Dick, and one by one they poke their heads out of the bedclothes again.'

'The Saint will look after them, won't he?'

'He will, and they will look after themselves, too. Tom Barker turns to Long Rachel and Little Dick turns to Milly Larkin, and they all fall to kissing, but there's no one for Minny Wilkin.'

'How sad!'

Tetty listened to the story and hugged her own bare sides in the dark like Minny Wilkin. Quiet minutes gradually filled the loft and for a while there was silence.

Then came another voice, but a sleepy one.

'Gweno, are you still flying?'

There was only a sigh in reply.

'Gweno, tell about the Saint. Tell about the Saint and the bird.'

Then Gweno's voice came quietly from her pillow.

'Long long ago . . . a long long long long very long time ago . . .'

'Yes, go on.'

'Before the abbey was built, before the brothers came, before there was a farm . . .'

'Was I here, Gweno?'

'No, indeed you were not. There was nobody here at all. And the Saint came to the island from the sea and he set foot on the rocks and he walked on the shore and it was hot then like it is now. The Saint was tired and thirsty because he had come a long way across the sea. Then he found a little bird in its nest which was as dry and weak as he was for lack of water. As dry as he was. Dry as dry . . . as dry as dry as dry . . .'

'Go on, Gweno.'

'And the Saint stamped on the rock with his foot and broke the rock open and a spring came out, all fresh clean water. And he took the bird from its nest for it was too weak to fly and put it by the spring and he let it drink as much as it could before he touched the water himself and when the bird had drunk from the spring it was quite better again and flew away happily. And the Saint stayed on the island and built the well over the place of the spring which became famous to all man- kind.'

Gweno's voice trailed off sleepily, and by now most of the girls were sound asleep. But Tetty's hands moved over her body as the waters against the island, wave upon wave, and they found the little bird in its nest and they too made it fly.

Beneath their window was a fruit tree with a ladder sticking up through it into the moonlight, and the orchard stretched away down a gentle slope to a fence which kept out sheep. Beyond the fence was a path that led from the abbey to the harbour.

While the girls were talking, Vane's boy met the Manciple on the path. He was startled by the sudden appearance out of the darkness of this squat figure whose flat skull sat so low in his thrown-back cowl that he seemed almost headless. He was carrying something in a bag, too, which he twirled as he walked so that the weight of it spun at the end of his fingers. It might almost have been his own small head that he was carrying.

'Where are you going to, boy?' he asked. 'Can't hear you. What did you say? Come out with it. What's your name?'

'Geoffrey, sir.'

'Well, Geoffrey?'

'I was going for a walk, sir.'

The Manciple grunted.

'Licking pies, rather,' he said mysteriously.

'I beg your pardon, sir?'

'You'll need a bag to catch coneys, boy,' said the Manciple, swinging his own bag against Geoffrey's breeches. The soft weight of it was unpleasant and made him twist aside.

'How's your bag, Geoffrey?' said the Manciple. He seemed to be amused by this conversation and went on his way, swinging his bag and laughing like the sound of two rubbed branches grating in a wind.

Geoffrey continued on his way to the harbour, looking down from the cliffs at the rocks below as he had done several times since they had first landed. He did not dare to go nearer. The horse could hardly be seen at first, but there was just enough moonlight reflected from the rocks to enable him eventually to make out its shape. He stared for a long time, until he was certain that the horse was now no longer moving its head.

'Oh, Saviour!' whispered Geoffrey. He was careful to prevent himself from weeping.

8

Early on the following morning Mrs Ffedderbompau fell out
of a tree while supervising the picking of fruit. One of the
girls had not been able to suppress a laugh as her mistress,
missing her footing, had let out a great shriek and for one brief
moment appeared to be reclining at sudden ease on her back
in the middle of the tree. But a second branch snapped,
and Mrs Ffedderbompau fell into the grass with a nasty
thud.

The girls were shocked, but one or two soon ran up to help
her. She was carried into the farmhouse, moaning in pain,
and put into her bed. Tetty was immediately sent to tell the
Abbot what had happened. But though she pulled at his bell
for six or seven minutes, he didn't appear. She knew that the
novices were not allowed to speak to her, and she was afraid
to speak to them, even though two of them appeared
together at the other end of the courtyard while she was
standing at the Abbot's door. After a while she returned to
the farm, feeling that she would be more help there.

The Abbot had woken early, with much on his mind. He
was irritated by the investigations of Vane, which threatened
not only to disturb his work but perhaps also to lead to
changes in its very foundation. Suppose Vane, in his con-
sideration of the efficacy of the holy waters, were irretrievably
to damage the well? Might there be any action forthcoming
from the Bishop as a result of anything adverse about its
administration conveyed to him by Vane?

The Abbot had slept on his right arm, and the pain of its

numbness was what had awoken him. Turning carefully, he moved the dead arm with his left hand from under his body, laid it on his chest and slowly massaged the life back into it. What, he reflected, if life could be similarly given back to a dead body?

What indeed was life? It was not the body, even though the body itself were preserved indefinitely. It was not motion, for motion could be suspended. Was it, after all, simply the spirit, whose location his long researches were designed to establish?

The body was like a house, whose single inhabitant might be impossible at any one time to find. You could move from room to room, even on one floor or around a single stairwell, and be forever entering the chamber just vacated by the object of your pursuit.

And what was this object? The Abbot had for a long time pursued it, but he could not say what it was. He dissected each part to understand its working, but finally each organ, each bone, each sustaining mechanism of tissue was revealed as little more than an empty room in a house that seemed to grow larger the more familiar you became with it.

This was the house, indeed, that must according to the text in Matthew be guarded against the thief who might come at any hour, the least expected. *Si sciret paterfamilias qua hora fur venturus esset, vigilaret utique et non sineret perfodi domum suam.* But the Abbot had ceased to be much interested in sin, and the image of the robber in the house came to mean something other than the Devil. Wielding the knife and laying aside the skin in layers from the flesh and packed muscles, he often felt himself to be the unexpected intruder. And where was the householder? No longer vigilant, for sure.

In his own house, the Abbot was not certain which role he

played. Sometimes he walked half-purposefully, half with designed carelessness, through the passageways of one of the wings as though to establish his right to be there. But the extent of these corridors and the strangeness of unvisited rooms often perplexed him: it seemed to him like another house, not his own, in which he must necessarily be not proprietor but intruder.

This feeling was increased by the real strangeness of some of the rooms he came across, rooms that he sometimes remembered using before and sometimes hardly felt that he had ever visited at all. He had only to turn left instead of the customary right on the third floor above his dining-room (at the head of the staircase that led from the ante-room to the dining-room, not the stairway by the fireplace) to find himself in a strangely dusty stretch of the house. He had been there unexpectedly just the week before, having taken the wrong turning without thinking, and had looked in fascination at rooms that had not been used since the days of his predecessor. He began by walking round the rooms, lifting the hangings and looking up chimneys and peering out of the tiny mullioned windows at unaccustomed views. Then he moved more quickly down the corridor, simply glancing into each room and if the door stuck hardly bothering to open it. His feeling was one of exasperation at not finding what he had come for, and then of perplexity when he reflected that he had not in the first place come for anything at all, but was wandering about by chance.

And yet he still felt in pursuit of something, and the not finding it (or was it a suppressed fear that he might indeed unexpectedly find it?) sent him scurrying down the next staircase in the general direction of the parts of the house that he knew.

Was the soul, he wondered, like this? A stranger in its own house?

He woke each morning with these thoughts, and hastened from his offices at the earliest opportunity to conduct his researches. At the hour when Tetty rang on his bell he had descended to his library where he was conscious that no sound could disturb him through fathoms of stone. He had it in mind to consult the Arabic authorities on the nature and function of the pineal gland, an organ which had naturally for some years been at the centre of his quest for the precise physical seat of the human soul.

The library was situated beneath his study, and was reached from a hidden staircase leading from behind a wooden panel in a small oratory adjacent to the study. He had converted the room to its present purposes many years before, to be secure from prying eyes. It had been a cellar, or some such. He could not remember. His tuns of Bordeaux lay elsewhere.

Being a cellar, and being damp, kept the books from drying and cracking, which he knew was a hazard. But their softness, the musty aroma and the fine organic bloom upon some of them gave him now and then cause for concern. He would take down a volume from one of the top shelves, little used (as he now did with the learned Avicenna), and find it clammy to his touch, almost as though the pores of the long-dead hide opened again and sweated at his touch.

The fear of the guardians of the word to yield their secrets!

The seat of the soul had to obey several conditions. Firstly it must be one; to the end that action of the same object that at the same time strikes two organs of the same sense should make no more than one impression on the soul, as for example, she might not see two novices carrying a bucket of water where there was only one. Secondly, it must be very near the source of the animal spirits, that by their means she might easily move the members. And in the third place, it must be moveable; that the soul causing it to move immediately might be able to determine the animal spirits to glide towards some certain muscles rather than others.

Conditions nowhere to be met with but in the little gland called pineal!

The pineal gland (or conarium) was situated between all the concavities of the brain, supported and encompassed with arteries which made up the *lacis choroides*.

'It is that *lacis*,' reflected the Abbot, hitching up his habit and resting one foot on the lowest shelf, 'that we may be assured is the source of the spirits which, ascending from the heart along the carotides receive the form of an animal spirit in that gland, disengaging themselves from the more gross parts of the blood.'

He turned several pages, but found nothing further to prompt his cogitations.

'From thence,' he mused, returning the book to the shelf and scratching his nose, 'they take their course towards the different muscles of our body, partly dependently, partly independently on the soul. As indeed the great author of nature has ordered it, with reference to the end he proposed to himself in the production of mankind.'

He must examine this gland again, he decided.

Before leaving his library he happened to place his hand against the rear wall, the only surface that was not filled with books. Usually a stone surface of this sort, in a room at this level, was cool and damp. But this was warm to his touch, like an oven at the very end of a baking day when the cinders could be raked out. And it was dry.

The Abbot was surprised at such an effect of the weather.

It was extraordinarily hot. Hotter than he had ever known it in his life. But to dry out a cellar! It was unheard-of.

Yet the library was not in fact dry. Indeed it seemed even more humid than usual. The air settled at the base of the Abbot's throat, heavy and irritant, as if it knew it was not of the quality to be safely admitted to the delicate palace of the lung. If he put a finger into the folds of his habit to press the hollow between his collarbones, he could feel the labour of his respiration like a pulse, and the dampness of the hot air made him wheeze like an old door.

Then he noticed where the dampness was coming from. Along the crevices between the lowest course of stones, knee-high, that supported the wall there trickled a constant ooze of viscous liquid. It glistened on the lower part of the wall and was sticky beneath his sandals.

He put a finger to it and cautiously touched the finger with his tongue. A dull, stony taste, not saline, but heavy. It was like some liquid that he knew, but he could not think what it was.

He was concerned for the state of his books but was distracted by a fit of coughing, and left hastily. There was too much to think about: the need for further dissection; the preparation of the senior novice for his forthcoming night of examination; the pacification of Vane; the remainder of his new sermon, and many other duties.

He did not hear of Mrs Ffedderbompau's accident until later.

9

'How much further?' growled Vane to the novice. His donkey stumbled frequently on the stony incline, and the jolting pained him. He had left behind his hat on account of the heat and now wished he were wearing it for the same reason.

The novice was the same one who had led the party from the boat two days before. He had said nothing then, and said nothing now. Vane watched his cowled figure mounting steadily ahead of him with increased displeasure. The only response he gave to Vane's question was to raise his arm and point ahead. He hardly seemed to be affected by the heat.

'Whereas I,' thought Vane to himself, 'might very well have been poisoned, I feel so ill.'

Geoffrey, wandering off the path and scrambling among the rocks and bushes, seemed to keep up with them without effort. He stooped every now and again to pick something, and presently came up to Vane with a handful of berries.

Vane shook his head. He was in no mood to eat anything, having eaten enormously that morning of a plate of meat produced in sly triumph by the Manciple personally. It was dark, sweet meat, three slices of it in a wooden dish, and Vane had wolfed it down as if he had not eaten for a fortnight. Now it lay uneasily on his stomach, like an animal twitching in a nightmare.

'Isn't the well over in that direction?' muttered Vane. 'I thought it was directly above the abbey? The abbey was built just below it, deliberately.'

'We are going to the cemetery first, sir,' said Geoffrey, with a purple mouth. 'The Abbot said we should go first to the cemetery.'

'Yes, yes, of course,' said Vane.

The cemetery was situated over the mountain, in the centre of the island, as though to secure the graves as far as possible from the danger of slipping into the sea and floating away. Or perhaps it was to ensure that the final resting-place of the pilgrims was in as elevated a position as possible to give them a dramatic advantage at the blast of the last trumpet call.

When they arrived, Vane held up his silver cross and blessed the place, which was a grassy mound cleared of bracken and thorn and ringed with a wall of stone. The grass itself was undisturbed, thin, dry and rusty, clustered on the graves. The stones were simple, and their inscriptions econo-mically though neatly carved.

While Vane moved among the rows, consulting his list, the novice stood by the little gate with his arms folded. Geoffrey took the donkey in search of water, but there was only one stream and that was dry, barely a smudge of darker earth streaking the scorched and crumbling heather.

The novice had learned, in a short space of time, that Vane was a person whom it was impossible to admire. He did not feel obliged to play any part in the checking of the graves, and took instead the opportunity to meditate.

He thought of a dream that he had had recently and which still remained vivid. The Abbot had appeared before him silently, while he was alone in his cell. The visit was un-expected and unannounced, and really he knew that the Abbot was long dead. He was not frightened by this, but accepted the mystery calmly as though the appearance was long-awaited and the Abbot had something important to tell him, some final piece of instruction to impart before his night of examination. There was great joy in the Abbot's damaged features. Some ordeal of his own had been overcome. He had been too timid to touch the Abbot's shoulder, though tenderly reaching for the crusts and pelt, the skin lifting in hardening slices of sores and gristle. His words were gentle: 'What is it?' The Abbot's almost unspoken answer was forceful, broad, deep, carrying the emotion of the encounter before it like a river in flood: 'Earth.' It was like the bestowing of a prize, a complete confrontation of the mystery, of origins, fortune, matter and destiny.

The novice remembered the answer as he watched Vane stooping above the last of the pilgrims, tucked up comfortably into the mountain, but it was his own question that lingered. 'What is it?' What was the 'it'? He knew that it was the question that lent the dream its significance.

And it was the embodiment of questioning in the ordered yet irritable motions of the sweating Vane that prompted the novice's ensuing meditation: 'It is quite elsewhere,' he thought, 'that the quantity of our devotion is measured, and we have no say in the matter. Meanwhile the censor continues to interrogate a dormitory of corpses.'

On their way to the well, Vane's mood changed. He became grim, confident, mildly exuberant.

'Three out of twenty-six,' he said, rocking steadily with the motion of the donkey as they walked along the gulf between the mountains.

Geoffrey was leading the animal. He looked back at Vane, as if to indicate a response. It would have been presumptuous of him to speak, but he knew well how to act as a conversational sounding-board.

'Only three graves of those I came to find,' said Vane. 'Twenty-three pilgrims are still unaccounted for.'

Geoffrey stroked the donkey's ears, which twitched together like a pair of warm shears.

'And the newest of the graves is a year old,' said Vane. 'Your sexton is out of work, eh, brother?'

The novice did not look back, and Vane gave a short laugh which turned into a belch. A shadow of nausea passed across his face, and he kept silent again till they came to the well.

The well filled a stone trough the size of three four-poster beds, and was roofed over. At one of the narrower ends, where light fell on it from the doorway, the water ran out over a small spout into a channel at the base of the trough where it flowed back into the darkness of the well-house.

The thread of water was almost motionless in its falling, except for a slight twist that blurred its smoothness, moving down the thin flow at a gentle pace like a hand idly stroking a lock of hair. It glittered in the shaft of the sun, and made a small sucking watery sound where it touched the stone and trickled away.

Vane slid off the donkey and ran up to the water, drinking noisily from his cupped hands. The novice merely dipped his finger to the wet stone and touched his forehead with it, and Geoffrey did the same. He was thirsty enough to follow Vane's example, but a sense of deference to their guide held him back. This ceremonious approach to the holy well didn't preclude later drinking, he felt.

Vane took little notice of what the others were doing, but entered the well-house. He had taken a small phial from his pocket, and now he filled this from the trough and sealed it with wax paper. He had been instructed to do this by the Bishop, but whether it was as a piece of evidence to be investigated, or whether it was for the Bishop's own use, he could hardly say.

There was a strange smell in the well-house, sweet beyond the mustiness of the confined space or the earthy taste of the holy seeping. As his eyes became accustomed to the darkness, Vane could make out the shape of a man in the water, half in and half out, his arms hooked back over the sides of the trough like a swimmer resting. The position looked so natural that Vane at first expected him to make some greeting, or a comment on the temperature of the water. But although the man's eyes were half open, he was clearly dead. Something brown dribbled from a corner of his mouth and drifted stickily at an angle from his chin to the water, like a fisher-man's line.

Vane ran out of the well-house, his gorge heaving. While Geoffrey and the novice went in to see what he had found, marvelling at his inarticulate murmurs and gesticulating, he bent over with one hand on his knee and vomited on to the grass.

It was not the seeing of the dead, for Vane had seen many, nor was it the unexpectedness. Rather it was the thought of consuming the death-fluids of the unfortunate pilgrim: his stomach, in which the morning's meat already maintained its shape, long after it should have decomposed, rebelled at the thought of combining them. And now all that he had eaten that day lay warm on the dry grass outside the well-house.

Feeling better, he stared in curiosity at the patch of vomit. He had heard of wells that effected great cures: wounds of impossible severity were healed, even the dead brought back to life. Why shouldn't the holy water he had swallowed have some effect upon the gobbets of flesh that lay before him?

He did not admit to himself the suspicion that the Manciple

had fed him his own horse, but if he imagined the half-digested fragments miraculously regaining some of the vital force that once animated them, it was as horse that he imagined it. Their only resurrection, however, was from his own stomach: their small stirrings before him were due to nothing more than gravity and the elasticity of the grass they lay on.

In the well-house, Geoffrey and the novice were trying to pull the corpse out of the water.

'Leave him,' said Vane, who could not at that moment face the problem of the removal of the body.

They each let go of the arms they were holding, and the dead pilgrim fell forward into the water. In this new position the body became half submerged, floating face down with arms extended, as though it were searching for something in the water.

'Leave him,' said Vane once more. 'I'd like the Abbot to see this.'

Rags attached to a thorn bush growing near the well-house hung dry and stiff from the branches, tokens of wounds long unwrapped in hope of cure. Where those wounds were now, and whether wrapped once more, was as uncertain as the cause of the man's death; and yet the hope that had brought them and him to the island was as undeniable as the horseness of horse, and who could say when hope first fades?

The path back to the abbey fell at a steady gradient, with the directness of an instruction on a diagram. Vane reflected that it would have been easier to have ascended by this route, which had obviously been marked out for frequent traffic, perhaps for the smooth piping of the water. The Abbot should go up in a cart and bring the corpse down, and then he would have some explaining to do.

10

'And what were you doing in the tree in the first place?' asked the Abbot.

'Picking apples,' smiled Mrs Ffedderbompau.

'A great woman of your age should not sit in trees,' said the Abbot.

He was sitting by her bed with his hands on his knees. On his face was such a helpless expression of concern that she could not stop herself from reaching out and clasping one of his hands with her own.

But even at that moment of meaningful touching, so potent for him that he imagined the feeling reversing itself like an echo and bestowing upon the sufferer an image of its infinite grace, the pain darkened her face. Then he knew that the barrier between them remained, no more forbidding than any like it at the boundaries of skin, but a barrier nonetheless.

Within the applied study of her pain she offered notions that might please him.

'We have had much to do with apples that has brought us to grief,' she said.

He made a deprecatory gesture.

'As for trees,' he said, lifting her hand and returning it to the pasture of its counterpane. 'When the fruit defeats us, there are always garlands.'

She raised her eyes in pleased expectation of an explanation.

'I was thinking of Apollo,' he said, 'the pagan god of poetry and healing.'

'Ah,' breathed Mrs Ffedderbompau from the depth of her

47

pillows, 'was he not the gentleman who chased his lady into a tree?'

'Love eluded him,' said the Abbot, 'but the laurel conferred the greater prize.'

'We must hope so,' she replied, 'but what did the lady think?'

'It is not recorded.'

'I thought not.'

The Abbot had no further observation to make on this subject, for it had come to seem inapposite. For whereas garlands become brittle, and are bestowed, the fruit is for the moment and to be taken. The comfort of the farm, the sense of bustle and order under the cool rafters, the appointed tasks and cheerful shared activity, these were due to the female response to the seasons and to what fittingly belonged to them. It was an absolute virtue of the sex, tested and proved in the full round of life. That other truth, belonging to gods, could not compete with it. For in the world of the farm, Daphne did not run and Eve knew only the moment when the fruit was ripe.

The Abbot had come to Mrs Ffedderbompau as both friend and physician, his smile of greeting accompanied by an involuntary glance of diagnosis. But she had waved him to a chair.

'It is inside that I am broken,' she had said. 'My limbs are sound, but incapable of direction, like a clockwork that is stopped.'

'Can you not move?'

'I am stopped from moving at the centre. The spring has snapped, here in the nest and cradle of life.'

And she had turned to the window in tears, as though it were the apple branches, the tops of which were to be seen there, that required her. As though that laden fruit were her only deprivation.

At intervals Tetty appeared with cool water in a wooden bowl, to bathe her forehead.

The Abbot instructed her to gather comfrey, for a poultice, but he could not find in his heart much enthusiasm for this remedy. The reddened contents of a jordan beneath the bed were indication enough of the gravity of Mrs Ffedderbom-pau's condition. Comfrey would have a struggle to cure it, and his patient understood as much.

'Brother Matthew would have prescribed comfrey,' she observed.

'And you are amused to find me doing the same?'

'Strangely enough, I think it is consoling. I have a great love of comfrey. And I loved Brother Matthew.'

The Abbot felt at that moment that he was the true inheritor, not only of the defunct Brother Matthew's role on the island, but of all the arts and failings of Apollo.

11

On his return he continued with his dissection. Being meticulous, he observed and made notes upon every aspect of the corpse worthy of such observation, as though chronicling the whole history and culture of a dead civilization.

'A large breast. Lungs not fungous, but sticking to the ribs and distended with much blood. A lividness in the face, as if he had a difficulty of breathing a little before his death.'

Institutions, laws, council-chambers, all deserted as by a plague, opened to the knife.

'Heart great, thick, fibrous and fat. The blood in the heart blackish and dilute.'

Roads, fields, prisons, factories, analysed on a table from which the liquids gathered and were channelled back into the corpse-pit.

'The cartilages of the sternum not bony, but flexile and soft. The viscera very sound and strong, especially the stomach.'

Every now and then the knife had to be resharpened on an oiled stone, and while it was being sharpened the same question played in the Abbot's head: 'Where is the private chamber of the ruling spirit?'

He supposed that the body was, as usual, that of a pilgrim. Perhaps it belonged to the departed soul of William Evans of Chester. Was it the last repository of all the human affection its earthly motions had warranted? Where now was the love of his dead wife for this grey, wet shape? And what had happened to the articulated flesh of the woman herself, loved in its turn?

He thought of the two souls, disembodied, in bliss. And experienced a wave of revulsion from a notion so palpably difficult to encompass. On to the conarium!

His investigation was interrupted by the ringing of the abbey bell, as if for divine service. It was not such an hour, he knew, and he suspected (rightly) the officious demands of Vane.

'Is there no other way to reach you, except by the great bell?' stormed Vane, when the Abbot appeared.

'I suppose not,' said the Abbot. 'Though no one except you would think of so peremptorily demanding me.'

Vane told him of their discovery of the dead pilgrim in the well. To the Abbot, who had only a moment before been cutting up a body that he presumed belonged to a pilgrim, such news was not sensational. But he listened with every appearance of attention and concern. The novice stood by, rapt in a contemplative silence beyond any possible division of loyalties.

'Isn't it clear,' asked Vane, 'that all my suspicions are justified? The well does not cure—far from it—and you do not bury your dead.'

'Brother Matthew once analysed the water from Lleuddad's well,' said the Abbot. 'He told me that there were substances that he could not identify. My opinion is that its properties are mysterious and inestimable.'

'It could not keep a pilgrim alive,' retorted Vane, 'let alone cure him.'

'If a man inhales water,' said the Abbot, simply, 'by being submerged in it, for a period of time, then there is very little that can cure him.'

'A period of time?' said Vane. 'You admit, then, that this man has been drowned for a period of time without rescue or burial?'

'It would appear so,' said the Abbot. 'Although you must understand that the well is not permanently supervised.'

'Why not?'

'The abbey cannot authorise worship at the well. It is not an altar.'

'But its sanctity is established. It has the Bishop's authority.'

'Indeed,' smiled the Abbot. 'I believe the twenty-sixth canon of Saint Anselm is of particular significance on this point, for it decreed in 1102: "Let no one attribute reverence or sanctity to a dead body or a fountain without the bishop's authority." Yes. We look to the Bishop to sanctify wells.'

'So?'

'Now you question its sanctity. You say it does not cure. It seems to me that the Bishop must make up his mind.'

Vane grasped the edge of the table with both his hands until the knuckles whitened.

'That,' he said icily, 'is precisely why I am here.'

'Oh, I understand that well enough,' returned the Abbot. 'But I am attempting to distinguish between well and altar. The Bishop has few doubts about altars, I imagine?'

Vane had no desire to continue debating with the Abbot. He had for some time reached the conclusion that he was not serious, and had decided that the best course was to humour him, and to remain watchful. He demanded that the Abbot make up a party to ride up to the well and to bring back the body of the dead pilgrim. There was some fuss about finding a third donkey which irritated him further, and he dispensed Geoffrey from further duties that afternoon, since he felt that one session with the corpse had been quite enough for the boy. Geoffrey went off gladly in the direction of the harbour, for dead bodies did not worry him and there was one, not human, for which he cared and for which he hoped that something, perhaps in the way of exequies, might even now be done.

When the party reached the shoulder of the mountain, and hurried into the well-house, they found the well empty.

'Trickery!' shouted Vane. He did not bother to wipe away the sweat which trickled down his face and gathered at his nose like rheum, as he leaned on the rim of the well and stared into the waters.

'The body was clinging to the side, you say?' mused the Abbot. 'And you dislodged it?'

Vane grunted assent.

'The well is much deeper at one end than you suspect,'

continued the Abbot. 'In fact, no one quite knows how deep it is.'

Vane ignored him.

'The body must have been removed,' he said.

'Perhaps it has been resurrected,' countered the Abbot, himself now exasperated at the temper and obtuseness of the Bishop's officious minion. 'You may report a wondrous and unexpected efficacy of the healing liquids of the well.'

Vane merely looked at him in blank wonder. The proposal, being of a totally different character from the suspected legerdemain on the Abbot's part, could not be entertained. But the Abbot's words for a moment entered his mind and did not seem ridiculous. They had a force beyond human argument, as would a voice from the rocky peak above them or, perhaps, tiny neighings in the grass.

The novice as usual stood apart by the doorway, converting the scene into a meditation for his book. As Vane and the Abbot peered into the water he thought to himself: 'The unknown trader, marooned once again after exhausting adventures and chained to the island by a malign invisible power, removes himself at will through native cunning and the borrowed influence of a magic fountain.'

12

Although the island was ringed with the blue of eyes, shaded here and there with elusive streaks of a darker colour, but altogether, as seen from the mountain, of a brightness to impel the gaze; nonetheless, at the sea's edge its appearance was oily, umber, repellant. The rocks that the tide periodically covered were smooth and humped, clad in skins of a slippery gelatinous weed. Between them the clefts swirled with the movement of longer tendrils in black water that never seemed still. A little further up the shore the boulders that were free of the attentions of the tide were baked paler by the sun and covered with lichens in random scribbles: ochre splashes and larger bisecting rings of bronze. This colouration, on grey slabs of varying sizes, had the strange consistency and persistence of a pattern. As he climbed over the rocks, Geoffrey picked at the crusty rings of dried fronds and crumbled them in his fingers.

He had seen Saviour's head and shoulders from the headland in just the same position as on the previous evening. From that distance the posture looked natural, even relaxed, as though the horse were sitting at ease and looking down the shore. Geoffrey was seized with a sudden hope that he might, after all, not yet be dead, and had made his way down to the rocks where the beast had leapt and fallen.

As he approached, he could hear above the lapping of the sea another, stranger, sound, like the wind in the tops of trees—only there was no wind. It came from the body of the horse which Geoffrey could now see was quite dead, for its haunches were already decomposed, leaving the spine arched like a flying buttress. Beneath it, heaped and massed within the collapsing bulk of the animal, was an army of maggots the volume of a broken sack of meal. He came closer and watched them with a sickened respect for this ferocious process of corruption: each maggot writhed and flopped in its effort to struggle free of the mass and to secure for itself a scrap of the decaying flesh to feed on, half of each white coiled body twisting blindly and reaching above the others for a hold that the air could not provide. Their movement was indistinct and hypnotic, for the eye, in attempting to observe the motion of every individual, failed to see more than the general heaving. It was like watching a single flake in a snowfall, and their sound was now like the gentle hissing of frying bacon.

The months that he had been in Vane's service seemed tedious and overlong, but those same months had seen the comparatively brief custody of Vane's horse. That friendship was now irrevocably ended, but the bondage to Vane stretched before him like a limitless sea in which there was only the vaguest chance of beaching on some redeeming and friendly island.

The pain of his loss of the horse now seemed to require some answering sacrifice, and his curiosity about the radical metamorphosis of death to require some ritual expression. Without forethought, Geoffrey thrust his spread hand into the heaving maggots.

For a moment the incredible warmth, like that of a freshly-baked loaf, was satisfying. The mysterious depths of the stirring mass, half-flesh, half-maggot, held and almost drew in his fingers as though they were spread drowsily beneath a downy pillow. But within a few seconds Geoffrey realised what he had done and withdrew his hand in disgust.

The maggots dripped from his fingers until he shook off the crawling glove in three whip-like movements away from him. Even then one or two still adhered to the skin, and one waved, crushed, from a fingernail. He daubed it on to a rock.

After that, he had to leave the place. He walked along the headland in a fury, thinking of all that he had left behind: his father, who could shoe a horse in fourteen minutes and who sometimes, when he was happy, sang after supper and danced stiffly on his toes behind the kitchen door; his mother, who could comb her hair out all round her head so that you could hardly guess where her hidden face was; his elder brother, who could catch a fish with his fingers; his younger brother, adept at beautiful selfish arguments.

His last memory was of him urinating dangerously in a patch of nettles and having to be carried to him to say goodbye, since Frobisher was in haste to get his cart to Hereford, and would not stay. 'Goodbye, Geoffrey.' The wet kiss had been planted on his nose, and months of service to the dry and energetic Vane had not replaced the memory of it. He had stopped writing letters home, because no one in his family could read, and the letters written for his mother by the curate bore no resemblance at all to her voice.

From the cliff he could now and then see small pebbly inlets, sometimes with caves, where the sea was able to lap the shore more gently than on the rocky promontories that predominated on the island's rough coast. He was surprised to discover one which had what looked like over a hundred yards of sand and a shelving beach where the tide curled idly, as if with relief at not being required to shoulder pillars of granite, or grunt and slobber over tiers of boulders. His first thought was to wonder why the boat from the mainland couldn't have beached here; then he saw the rocks ranged right across the mouth of the bay, crowding thickly like the heads of farmers at a fair gathered to watch the main event of the afternoon. And on the sand, as if in response to such expectation, there were four brown cows.

Geoffrey had not seen cows on the island before. These were of such a rich sandiness, sandier than the sand itself, as though by placidly standing on it they had drained it of all colour, that they had the air of belonging wholly to the little cove. They formed a small procession, ambling through the foam

that seeped away at the crest of each wave and leaving steam-
ing dumps of their dung at intervals.

At their head, dancing before them, leading them with
arms raised as though they were on invisible ribbons, was a
girl dressed in grey. There was a lightness in her bare feet and
a carelessness in her manner that somehow set her apart from
the animals in her charge.

Geoffrey thrilled to see this theatre of cows and descended
from the cliff along little brambly rabbit paths to get a better
view. The girl continued her dance as if she had not seen him.

Sometimes she faced them, walking backwards on her
toes and directing their movements. Sometimes she ignored
them, striding ahead with her arms raised sideways, head
down, observing the pad-pad of her feet and the momentary
space of her toe prints in the wet sand. Geoffrey cautiously
walked up and followed, like a fifth cow.

The girl spoke:
'Mulican, Molican, Malen, Mair,
Dowch adre'r awrhon ar fy ngair.'

'What did you say?' called Geoffrey from behind the
ambling rump of the last cow. But the girl made no answer.

'Are you a fairy?' he asked, with a respectful grin.

She darted him a quick, interested, warning glance while
at the same time pretending not to have noticed him.

'Where are you taking these cows?' he called.

She laughed.

'Into the sea!'

'Do they live in the *sea*?'

She laughed again, and twirled round on one foot.

'Do *you* live in the sea?'

At this, she looked directly at him with real amusement.

'Oh yes,' she said. 'At the bottom of the sea.'

They walked on together in silence, and when she suddenly turned and walked back through the following cows, Geoffrey followed at her side.

'Then you *are* a fairy,' he claimed.

'Think so, do,' she said. 'And if I were, where would my mother's daughter be now, then?'

He shook his head, smiling.

'Why,' she said, 'with the Tylwyth Teg themselves. Bound with ropes of gossamer and carried off to live with the fair family. And I to take her place.'

'Is that so?'

'Well, why should fairies drudge? It can't be so, for the fair family have the bees and creatures to do their small service. Why should they live with folk?'

'So you aren't a fairy?'

'No more than you are a brother. Or have you come to take orders?'

'Never,' said Geoffrey. 'I would rather be out of here, you can be sure of that.'

'The brothers hope for a great reward,' she said, as if he should consider her information carefully before making such a rash decision as to leave the island. 'If they are ordained they will live for ever.'

'Do you believe that?' asked Geoffrey.

She thought for a moment.

'No,' she replied. 'But they must be quite beyond this world, and if you can get quite beyond this world, beyond sleeping and eating and cows and grass and sky and all of it, then . . .'

'Then what?' asked Geoffrey.

'Just then,' said the girl. 'And if.'

'And what can there be beyond?'

'Oh, I don't know,' she said. 'What do *you* think?'

He looked at her looking at him, all eyes and hair, and the blood drained out of his cheeks and into his ears and he could not imagine at that moment anything at all like beyond, for it was all now, cows and grass and sand and sky and smiling lips.

13

For days Mrs Ffedderbompau watched the pair from her window, Tetty walking in the orchard, smiling and twisting the ends of her long hair, Geoffrey at her shoulder, talking of something or other. Or the two of them on the hill below the path, outlined against the sea, walking at that slight distance which results from intense conversation.

She sent Tetty for mushrooms, for which in her broken state and fever she felt a slight craving. When the girl appeared in the orchard with the basket, Geoffrey was as usual with her, walking just behind her, with one arm extended and the hand on her shoulder. The manner of walking, at once proprietorial and tender, stirred echoes within her, but of precisely what, she could not say.

From that moment she decided that she knew very well that she would not recover. And in that moment of knowing that we must know that we know, or else we might as well not know, there came to her suddenly and blindingly all that she had till then not fully known.

Or had she once known it? Was it perhaps that now understanding itself had to suffice and could not issue in action?

In the hot drench and prickle of the bedclothes she could not move in, the thoughts cast masterful shadows like imaginary limbs. They moved about the room behind her eyes, as if ready to pounce upon the innocent and vulnerable surfaces, wood, linen, glass, and press them into service. It was memory asserting the perpetual rights of experience, as she willed a cupboard to open, a cloth to be unfolded, a liquid to be poured.

Did it matter whether or not these things happened?

She thought that what had happened once couldn't be undone and was good for all time, that what was going to happen, was indeed at that moment happening, was perfectly as good as anything else that ever had.

Did it matter to whom these things had happened, were happening, or were going to happen?

She felt, mysteriously, that it didn't matter at all. For what she knew that she knew was certain as it could be, and what she didn't know was not in question at all.

By concentrating on one thing, she not only established that thing, but avoided the trouble of having to establish any more than that thing.

She began with the basket, and the hand through it that grasped its further rim lightly, the handle on the forearm, the empty woven bulk resting on the hip. Placed on the grass it awaited its filling.

Fill it!

Behind shut lids her eyes scanned the darkness as if it were greenness, searching for the tell-tale pattern of white. No, nothing so much as a pattern, but more like the trail of drops from a full bowl of milk carefully carried. And no, not so much white, as bone or wool was, misleading the eye, but the dull living colourless curdled colour of spider eggs, round like them, too. But hard and motionless in the grass, neither struggling to hide nor survive, quiet and yet signalling proudly, both a promise and a surprise with their tight unborn

scent of almonds, urine and milk. Webs, roofs, babies . . .
What were they, neither plant nor animal? She filled the
basket quickly with the fat curled buds, which rested against
each other companionably, respectful of contact, bowed and
nodding together in a gathered resignation, uprooted palaces
with the glorious savour of the fields upon them, their lintels
flecked with soil.

Too quickly, alas; an unlikely bounty. For try as she could,
she could see nothing else but useless fragments: a finger and
thumb at the thick base, pressing back the fronds, easing its
root; lips half open with the eagerness of the task; the plucking,
the deliverance. And so the basket filled. And she was not
inside Tetty's head at all, but inside her own. The fragments
of another's life were too clearly borrowed to be real.

The mushrooms were brought to her at last, but they weren't
the ones she had imagined. Some were taken to be simmered,
but she found she couldn't eat them. The rest were left in a
bowl in her room, where for a time their fragrance cast a spell.

'They are drying into the air,' said the Abbot when he saw
them.

There could be no reply to this, unless it were to complain,
with an air of comedy that weariness and pain could all too
easily dispel, 'and so am I.' She quite wanted to say other
things, some of them of mild importance indeed, things that
would not normally be said, and might not be said even now
at this late hour of life unless some courage could be found—
or the right moment. What were the subjects of these remote
communications? Geography and accident, the power of
sacraments, unspoken love, time and death, celibacy and
widowhood. What suitable occasion might be found to air
them? A deathbed. Only a deathbed? And would anyone
listen even then?

In the end Mrs Ffedderbompau decided to raise a more theoretical issue.

'Why,' she asked, 'am I inside myself and not somewhere else?'

The Abbot smiled faintly, his hands on his knees, leaning back in the uncomfortable chair. He was prepared for kind words, unusual feelings, even for confessions, efforts at truth. But her question was too close to his own inquiries to be easily pursued.

'I am a victim of what I can see, feel, hear,' she continued. 'But why should I be?'

'Why, indeed?' murmured the Abbot, looking at the place where her jaw became her ear and was framed with falling hair that was also crushed into the pillow.

'I don't blame you for not listening,' thought Mrs Ffedder-bompau, and she smiled a smile which the pain made the more radiant.

'How is your glow worm?' asked the Abbot.

'Ah,' said Mrs Ffedderbompau. His question was like a space on a table on which she could put down a heavy load. She had much to tell him about the glow worm he had found for her. 'I put her into a small thin box, such as pills are usually sent in, and between eleven and twelve last night I saw her shine through the box very clearly on one side, the box being shut.'

'Remarkable,' said the Abbot.

'I put white paper into the box, and the worm into the paper: it shone through the paper and box both.'

'She is a beacon of the hedges,' said the Abbot. 'The blown embers of Nature's dying fire.'

'But in the morning, about eight of the clock,' went on Mrs Ffedderbompau, 'she seemed dead, and holding her in a very dark place, I could see very little light, and that only when she was turned upon her back and by consequence put into some voluntary motion.'

'And now?' enquired the Abbot. 'How is she now?'

'Look for yourself,' said Mrs Ffedderbompau.

The Abbot did look.

'Why,' he laughed, 'she is walking briskly up and down in her box, shining as clearly as ever!'

Mrs Ffedderbompau laughed too.

'Yes!' she exclaimed, eagerly conspiring with him in pleasure at the observation, as though there were nothing else worth serious comment.

14

The windows of the cells were so small and high that the moon simply cast its ghostly patches on the ceilings without generally illuminating the sleeping shapes and their few possessions. And yet the outlines seemed quite clear in the half-darkness; the scrubbed bowl, the scowling cherubs at the shoulders of an oratory, the metal clasps of a book on a small table.

The novice who was shortly to undergo the night of examination reached out his hand and touched one of the clasps. His book was not finished, and he thought it might never be finished. The reflections in it of things as they really were could be no more, he decided, than insufficient reflections of things only as they seemed to be, reflections of reflections, moonlight patches at a pathetic remove from the sun.

Down the central passage between the rows of cells one of the brothers walked with a candle. His shadow, slanted and gigantesque before him, wavered and retreated as he moved forward.

The novice, lying on his cot with his hands clasped on his chest, saw the light from the candle through the crack above his door. He thought:

'Fire, whether near or distant, is all that we have to represent the illumination of the spirit. Its light passes fitfully over the darkened surfaces which are neither here nor there without it.'

After a while the light outside his room was gone, and he thought about the coming examination. For him it was like the lighting of a candle made ready for the testing touch of an external flame and required to bear it steadily against all wind of doubt and trial. The candle had not created its flame, and could preserve it for no longer than the length and thickness of the wax allowed, but for a lifetime the light was bestowed and he must prove its worthy guardian.

The flame danced upon the liquid tip of the wax as if in despite of the only substance that could give it life. It was tethered there, like the last leaf on a tree blasted by the storm. The novice thought:

'The spirit struggles to be free, vain as the wave struggling to attain the shape of a horse, or a horse struggling to fly.'

And he gave out a great cry in the solitude of his cell.

None of the monks did more than stir slightly in their sleep, for they were dead tired with the unaccustomed labour of excavating the stone conduit at the brow of the mountain near the Saint's well. Under Vane's direction they had worked for two days and revealed a passage hollowed from the giant blocks of stone that took the overflow of the well at a steady gradient down its cylindrical channel, wide enough for the passage of bodies, and polished smooth to speed their descent. The monstrous pipe of stone was set into, and indeed constituted the basis of, the path that led down from the well to the abbey. At intervals Vane ordered the monks to dig away at the cropped turf and top-soil to establish the continuation of the chiselled boulders beneath.

Torn between hatred of the island and a desire to get to the bottom of its mysteries, Vane would gaze out to sea as the monks bent to each new task, as if the appearance of the boat from the mainland were an expected signal for him to cease his commands, draw his investigations to a close and return to the Bishop.

But the boat did not come, and he continued to work the silent monks as though they were animals. The Abbot thought it wise to give him the authority to do so, and the monks, stooped all day in the heat, could think it no more than their duty to obey.

15

When the milk was solid enough, Tetty cut it with a knife and the cut bled whey. She made parallel cuts and the milk quivered. She could just tip the heavy bowl, making each scar of milk budge. She then made cross-cuts until the surface of the milk was a mesh of squares. Another girl helped her to turn the contents of the bowl into a basket, a tumbling mass of slippery strips, the whey draining away.

They were crumbling handfuls of sage into the cheese when Geoffrey came in with news of the excavations.

'The channel leads right up to the Abbot's house,' he said,

helping them to hang the dried bunches on to the hooks in the rafters.

'So?' smiled Tetty.

'Vane thinks the Abbot is stealing the bodies of the pilgrims.'

'Why, who could he be stealing them from?'

Tetty put her hands lightly on Geoffrey's shoulders and jumped down from the chair she was standing on.

'I don't understand you,' said Geoffrey.

'Don't you?' said Tetty, putting the tip of her finger to his nose.

'He's stealing from the pilgrims.'

'What would the pilgrims want with their bodies when they're dead? Anyway, you can't steal something from itself.'

'Why not,' persisted Geoffrey.

'You could steal a gold watch from a house,' said Tetty, 'but you couldn't steal a gold watch from a gold watch.'

'This is silly,' said Geoffrey, 'and I'm exhausted.'

He sat down on the cool stone bench that was built down one side of the dairy, leaning his head back against the wall. Tetty gave him a piece of bread, but after one bite he put it down on the stone beside him.

When all the cheese was draining, and the basins were being scoured, there was a noise outside like a sharp intake of breath. Geoffrey opened his eyes in time to see two of the older girls disappearing from the dairy, one carrying a knife. He looked questioningly at Tetty, who was looking out of the door. When she hurried out too, he followed her.

The outer door was closing. Or was it opening? As the girl with the knife passed through she confronted the Maniciple tying his donkey to the porch. Or was he untying it?

'Who was that person who just left?' he smirked. 'Someone I've not seen before, I think.'

They looked around, but there was no one.

'There,' said the Manciple. 'He went round the corner, into the yard.'

The girl who was carrying the knife had it raised and held out in front of her bodice like the handle of a pan. She kept it there.

'You seem alarmed,' he continued. 'Was it an intruder?'

No one said anything. Tetty and the second girl went into the scullery, where they found a child hiding in the corner between a cupboard and the wall. Her face was pale, and her eyes were wide and bright, but she was not crying.

At the insistence of the Manciple they searched the yard, but found no one, nor expected to. The Manciple shrugged, and looked with amused hostility at Geoffrey.

'Your Master is looking for you,' he said.

'Is he?' returned Geoffrey.

'I believe so,' said the Manciple absently, gazing at his nails.

Tetty buttoned the child's dress and led her into the dairy. The Manciple was provided with the loaves he had come for and left the farm, his donkey's panniers full. The girls resumed their work.

'I would kill that man if you wanted me to,' said Geoffrey. 'I'd cut little squares out of his ugly face.'

One of the girls laughed as she filled a pail, but Tetty said nothing. He tried to talk to her about other things, but she wouldn't speak. After playing with a mousetrap for a few minutes he left and returned to Vane.

In the afternoon Mrs Ffedderbompau held the lottery. Her curtains were drawn against the sun, and she could barely turn her head towards the door when the girls filed in. Some of the younger ones giggled and held their noses, and they were sent away. Blodwen had brought the bowl with the stones in it, and Mrs Ffedderbompau directed each of them to take the stones in turn until there was only one left, and it was Gweno's turn to take it. The others, who had been picking their stones out eagerly, now lost interest. They put their stones back into the bowl and left the room one by one, looking at Gweno with wonder, curiosity and a new respect.

When they were alone, Mrs Ffedderbompau motioned her to come closer to the bed. Gweno obeyed, although the smell was so strong.

'Child,' whispered Mrs Ffedderbompau. 'Let me see you as you were made, uncovered.'

Gweno stood uncertainly.

'Go on with you, slow thing. Take off your clothes.'

Gweno undid her dress, pulled it off her shoulders and let it fall to the floor, standing in its crumpled folds as clean and naked as a peeled stick. The signs of her sex stood on her innocent body like the marks of punctuation that betray meaning in an unknown language, the most common yet most secret code, the very arrows and targets of nature. And Mrs Ffederbompau sighed for the frail beauty of these indications of nature's hopes.

'Do you know, child, what it is that you will have to do?'

Gweno nodded.

'I don't believe you do.' Mrs Ffedderbompau sighed again. 'But it will be explained to you. Remember, my dear, that the novice's ordeal is partly a ceremony, a traditional celebration of the meaning of his ordination with tokens of the new powers he pretends to, and it is partly a real test of those

68

powers. And in all that he has renounced and in all that he has become, he is a true mirror of the Saint.'

Gweno lifted a corner of her fallen dress with her bare toe. Her eyes remained lowered with what mixture of sullenness, shame and boredom Mrs Ffedderbompau could not say.

'Keep the Saint in mind, my dear,' she said. 'The Saint guards our spirit, and restores it when the body is assailed.'

And Gweno, one lock of dark hair falling across her lowered face, thought of the dry bird and the broken rock and the terrible rotting dead private soiled smell of Mrs Ffedderbompau.

16

The shelves of the Abbot's library were covered with coin-sized patches of fungus the colour of raw liver. Those that were most developed were raised from the wood and could be turned aside with the fingernail to reveal greenish spores on their underside. When the Abbot tried to rub them off the shelves, he found his hands stained as if from the grease of door-hinges.

Curious! He scraped at the fungus with a corner of his habit. The cleaned wood seemed fresh and slippery, with a twiggy smell, and the occasional knot oozed gum. He had done nothing about the stony seeping from the walls, and now his sandals slithered about in the dirty veils of moisture on the flags, and the pediments of the wooden shelves were soaking up the liquid from the floor.

He was putting the finishing touches to his sermon, and had needed to consult some books. In any case, the sound of Vane's hammering and digging disturbed him and he wanted to escape from it. Vane had already traced the channel to an exterior wall, and had now excavated half the courtyard beneath his study. Stripped to the waist, he led the operations with a single-minded fervour. The last view the Abbot had had of him was as he lowered himself into the opened conduit some thirty feet below the window. It almost looked as though he were wriggling into a bed, pulling the Abbot's house over him like a blanket.

It always seemed possible to retreat further and further into the house to escape from intruders. Although turning left at the end of every corridor should have brought him back to his starting-point, it never did, and staring up the broad chimneys never brought a view of sky. The library, though a cellar, had cellars beneath it, and those cellars had access to rooms that were not cellars and which the Abbot had never seen. The humidity at the centre of his house seemed to be not due to the weather, but to be self-generating, like the property of a living organ. The library, dank, acrid and awash, became at once this organ's necessary manifestation and its secret function. The words it contained were closed from immediate view, nourished by the structured textures and surfaces that contained them.

The Abbot gently stroked the supple leather of the book he was reading. He fancied it yielded beneath his palm like the flank of some peaceable grazing creature. Could leather be cured of its curing? Could the sightless hides be reassembled, clasps turn to bells, the branded spines grow tails again?

He would lose first those books bound in vellum, for the bindings would turn back to stomachs and digest the contents. Or the shelves would grow into a hedge and keep out the hand that reached for knowledge.

He replaced the book while he still had access to the

shelves, before its covers might twist from his grasp with new-born awkwardness, trailing from embryonic gums a voided spittle of silent language.

17

He had not forgotten Mrs Ffedderbompau, but his visits had less and less use, and his mind could not reach her. She, for her part, could no longer even attempt to project her will upon the world she imagined. Even the world she saw, a dim arc of webs and beams, had nothing about it worth ordering. To be carried away, like a pet, in the folds of a garment: that was an objective indeed. If she could ride, a mite or a fairy, on the Abbot's left ear, clinging to a tuft of his hair! The spirits of the dead would have a short life of this sort, she reflected, aunts perched on the shoulder, a grandfather tucked into a sleeve like a handkerchief. Who would be lumbered with these crumbs of matter, themselves hoarding a distant army of fore-bears? Washed away with useless flakes of skin, fingernails, moisture, hairs, the whole world a litter of discarded recept-acles of eternal life all as dry as the husk of glow worm, starved in its paper box.

She concentrated her attention now on the perhaps doubt-ful existence of the throbbing effigy of discomfort that used to be her body. Experience told her that if she moved her arm she would find a cooler surface of the bed, but she was too weary to do more than lift the middle fingers of her hand, a gesture symbolising the awareness of the passing of time as in talking or waiting, a gesture that indicated or demanded the exercise of a barely-won patience. But this was a private piece of manual rhetoric, conducted beneath a blood-stained sheet. After a moment her hand was still.

She felt now beyond the disaster that had befallen her, beyond her nature and age, or any age she had ever been. And so she felt less and less sure of having any identity at all. Was it Gweno she had sent away, with her chaperones, to play her part in the novice's night of examination, or had she gone herself and was Gweno left dying here? She could easily think (indeed, some days since had hoped) that she might be carried in her bed to the abbey, borne on the shoulders of the brothers in the folds of her soft cortège, to observe the dedication, the humiliation, the drenching, the sermon, the processsion with the witnesses to the chamber.

The sermon in particular she would have dearly loved to hear, not for its theme (which by tradition concerned some aspect of the efficacy of the Saint) nor for its truth alone, but for the truth as understood by her friend the Abbot, so solemn and shy in his dealings with the world as she had lived it, but possessing a wisdom which she craved, and a nature which she half knew she loved.

The whisperings from the dairy below, the muffled din of crockery, the slight scrape and jar of benches as the harvest girls finished their supper—these and other more distant sounds of the farm were converted in her mind to the sounds of the congregated brothers in the abbey. She imagined the Abbot ascending the pulpit, his lips slightly compressed in concentration, the beard mingled with the dark folds of his habit, his hands reaching to grip the rim of the stone pulpit, and her heart suddenly fluttered and lurched in a full knowledge of what she was leaving and what in her full life she had most lacked.

To the dark and silent room she voiced her last words, a

rebuke to the emptiness about her, a challenge to the ceremonies that at the same moment were elsewhere taking place:
'We have failed to make the little bird fly!'

Her mouth stayed open, a thread of moisture between the
lips. In its absolute stillness her face seemed smaller, harder,
more beautiful, like a sudden relic of itself, almost lifesize. It
was as though the curtain of motion and colour had been
momentarily lifted so that the reality behind it could be
appraised, and the mechanism, though found to be irrevers-
ible, was a wonder for ever to the hushed audience of sur-
rounding objects. And so the Abbot began his sermon.

18

*Brothers, I show you here a mushroom by which you shall learn
about flying. And in my other hand is my text from Ezekiel xiii.20:
'Wherefore thus saith the Lord God; Behold, I am against your
pillows.' Be mindful of our brother who is brought before us in the
image of the blessed Lleuddad, bearing the pains and scourging of the
Lord. Hold him in your eyes and hear my words.*

*The mushroom is falsely named, you will say, for in it there is not
much room, but little room. Yet I say there is* multum in parvo,
*much room in little. In the narrow beams of this soft room there is a
savour; as in the leaves of this holy book there is a Saviour, whom we
may also breathe in at our nostrils and make much room for in our
souls. And our souls are like the mushrooms of the fields,* multum in
parvo, *an infinity of God's insufflation in a small rotundity of skull,
where little savour is not less than all the savour there is; for the
Saviour once sniffed is the true savour by which we distinguish life
from the corruption about it.*

Which of us can distinguish the savour of life from the savour of corruption? Brothers, the stink of the deathbed is sweet with the memories of a life that folds its wings; the savour of the fungus survives the rot of the stump or dunghill. Wherefore we gather in the fields these buds of the earth which like miracles appear, white with folded wings. However, these wings are not folded up, but to be unfolded as we are to be unfolded. From the soil the life thrusts upwards to the heavens; the soil itself thrusts, as souls thrust. The mushroom, bred of no seed, is soil only; the soul is only soil, and man is corruptible dust, though full of seed.

If a man is broken on the wind so that the pouch of his seed breaks, and if the air carries his image, it is no great matter. What is this, brothers, do you call it a motive? I call it merely wind and air, the idle movement of nothing, like water stirred by the hand. And all that is stirred must settle in time.

Therefore the desire to fly is a false desire of parting from the earth, our soil and nature, and the bed of our corruption. As the prophet cried: 'Woe to the women that sew pillows to all armholes, and make kerchiefs upon the head of every stature to hunt souls!' So the prophet shunned women, and hid his seed, so as not to hunt souls, for his soul's growing was the soil's growing that puts up the saviour in a little room that is self-bred of the soil. 'Wherefore thus saith the Lord God; Behold, I am against your pillows, wherewith ye there hunt the souls to make them fly, and I will tear them from your arms, and will let the souls go, even the souls that ye hunt to make them fly.'

A man cannot put himself above the soil of his germination and generation, no more than can a stone. Brothers, if you say a flower flies, I say it flies only on its root. If you say a bird flies, I say it flies only on its root, which is the foot with which it rests on the earth. The mountain lays its head in weariness, and the bird must tumble; bones return to the soil; and man is dust.

Brothers, remember the story of Lleuddad and the bird which flew above the island when the island was a stone. The Saint was weak with thirst and likely to die, and he looked on the bird which soared above him, drinking up the clouds, and he wished to be a bird. But while he wished to be a bird the island was dry, for the bird flew out of reach and drank up the clouds. Then Lleuddad fell back on the parched earth to die, and no longer wished to be a bird; whereupon the bird straightway fell to the ground, and where it fell broke the ground and a spring bubbled up out of the ground which the blessed Lleuddad drank and was saved.

What is the temptation that every monk must put behind him? It is the temptation to forget that he is dust. It is the temptation to fly.

Remember that spending with women is a struggle from roots, an attempt to fly. A man exalted of woman is a man who tries to fly. Free of the soil, the millions swarm; lip touches lip, restlessly seeking rest. Over the soil they move, finger to finger. Touch mysteriously propels them, endlessly, as though the soil does not wait.

Remember that spending with women is a struggle from roots, an an attempt to fly. A man who uses the grape is a man who tries to fly. There are shadows cast by no fire, and meaningless laughter, and the room is not still.

Remember that uttering strange words that drift in the wind is an attempt to fly. A man who cannot keep his silence is a man who tries to fly. The sounds emerge as from a wood which to enter were to be lost for an afternoon.

Therefore, brothers, I say remember the soil, and be secret, tread soberly and know not women. Be mindful in this of our Saint of blessed memory, Lleuddad, whose bones in the soil nourish our life on this island. Let his example then be a beacon to this novice, our brother, who lies here before us. He has announced his kinship with the dust, and on the dust he is prone. He figures the worm that is in each of us, our beginning and our ending. Amen.

19

When he had finished his sermon, the Abbot was ashamed, because he knew he had lied. 'It is no wonder,' he said to him/self, as the women led the novice away for his trial, 'that I am misunderstood. I hardly understand myself, for that is not what I meant to say at all.' He was disrobed, and then returned to his study where he sat quite silently in the dark, the sweat dampening the fringes of his beard.

Beneath him, working without light in the dank heat of a narrow stone space which was neither vertical nor horizontal, neither cellar nor foundations, was Vane. He slithered on stone slabs that were slimy with calcification, and waded in troughs that disappeared into walls so shallow that the space seemed all flooded ceiling. It scraped his stooping back and dropped sodden scales and blisters of distilled stone into his hair.

And all the while the spring water from the mountain ran in a determined current round his ankles. 'It's flowing here on purpose,' thought Vane. 'It's as though the Abbot's house was built here to receive its tribute of corpses.'

He did not believe that the Abbot was a cannibal but nor could he explain what happened to the bodies of the pilgrims. His investigation had rapidly turned into a particular investigation of the Abbot, against whom many charges could, it seemed, be made. The mismanagement of the well now looked like being the least of these. There was, for example, the rumour of his relationship with a woman at the farm, and of heresy in his doctrines. But Vane did not understand the Abbot's remarks, and suspected him of being an idler, whimsical in his isolation from any true religious discipline, or from any congregation that looked to his word. And where indeed was the community that Vane had expected to find? There was a handful of novices only, scarcely more than boys, no older than the girls who worked on the farm and probably their brothers. Were there no ordained monks? Were there no men of experience, wisdom and probity? Ordinations took place, he knew, for there was to be one that very day.

At least, it appeared to be intended to be an ordination, though from all accounts the forms of the ceremony were very strange. He had just begun to speculate on the fate of the island's novices and to try to link it in some logical way (it seemed to insist itself strangely, to propose itself almost as a puzzle) with the fate of the island's pilgrims, so near solution, when his foot met not slippery stone, shelving beneath a foot or two of water, but more water. Suddenly without warning he was up to his chest. Reaching for a handhold in the stone he found none, and could not keep his balance. Scrabbling in panic beneath the water he found himself clutching (could it be?) limbs, hair, fingers. In his alarm, reaching for the non-existent hold that would keep him upright, he lost his balance in the water entirely and was attracted to the soft bodies in the corpse pit, wafted and bumping down to them as though the well gathered and guarded its treasure in assemblies and lodges; drifting, sleeping, wrinkled shapes. Trying to push away from them only drew him nearer, his palms repelling surfaces that attracted and lingered, rolling over as if for the inspection of his shut eyes, till his breath gave out and he became a corpse himself. The question of the unordained novices remained open. He was transformed, but unblessed.

Geoffrey, instructed to guard the entrance of Vane's excavations against the inquisitiveness of the novices, now that secrets seemed close to being revealed, heard nothing of these events. He sat on a warm stone in the evening light, and the few monks near him told their beads as they faced the challenging mysteries of their brother's ordeal in the chamber above, mysteries cast by lamps lit early, in shadows, at the blank window. Geoffrey looked up, too, and wondered what was being required of the young man who had so silently and assiduously conducted them about the island during the past few days. He had asked Tetty, who at first pretended to keep a secret, but had at last admitted that she did not know. The older women were forbidden to talk of it, and the girls' games, which frequently centred on the ordeal, were muddled compilations of fiction and rumour. From one corner of the room to the other, an epic diagonal, without touching the floor, but clinging to the walls, on bedrails, chests, eaves, anything; in contrary motion, passing at the window, giggling, bodies against bodies; perched for rest, sweating, legs kicking and dangling; in whispers in cupboards: 'I'd like to die with them.'

When the novice's chest was unbound, the burrs and knots of grasses unfolded on the skin, the tight stalks springing free, falling away as the sweat dried, dropping to the bed sheets. The ulcers stood shyly on his body, like mouths about to speak. New candles burned in the room, sweet steady light in the still air illuminating the comings and goings of the women, casting shadows on the bed curtains. Gweno was washed, and laid in the bed; the cords were arranged across their bodies; water was sprinkled.

They might have been corpses there, or models for funeral effigies. Only Gweno's eyes, swivelling as if by ingenious clockwork in her otherwise still face, betrayed the ordinary curiosity of life. All else was stasis and resignation as the women strewed the chamber with herbs, drew the curtains and left on noiseless feet. What was the ordeal? Was it in, or was it out of, the bodies so laved and arranged together? To what was the body a challenge? For what absent lord did the tenant guard the house in his care?

The novice moved one finger against the sheet, as if to test his ability to control his limbs. His eyes became used to the darkness. 'The real nature of a test,' he reflected, 'is that we do not know what is required of us. And yet would the false hero, unable to drag the sword from the stone, survive the ordeal through knowing his inability to perform the task and therefore not attempting it? Only the basest villain, common beyond the escapist dreams of a threatened king, would pass by the stone in sublime ignorance.'

Within the linen cube of the bed-space the living shapes of the present made the demands that always belong to the present. A cheek, neck and shoulder claimed their exclusive right to measure the unbearably slow passing of time, insisting that their power over the attention was incomparable with any such power once possessed, or to be possessed. The novice knew, also, from instruction, that the ordeal belonged to the present; that its character was of a requirement of decisions and performance of the moment; that knowledge of the appropriate time of the test was a natural faculty of the pre-pared novice, not foreseen, but patent in its own natural course. If he shut one eye, the novice could see twenty toes and the bed hangings; if he opened that eye and shut the other, he could see the hill of bosom, the spread of hair and the whites of eyes looking at him in wonder. He lay still as an island, shutting first one eye and then the other. Gweno giggled, and turned the giggle into a hiccup. The air was close in the bed. A drop of sweat ran down the novice's cheek from his temple and settled in his collar-bone. The presence of the girl stirred half-realised memories of childhood, when night was at once a threat to the nest and a huddled shelter from that threat, when the sky rolled above in its courses and sleep was content to resign the human will to the moon and stars, which thundered silently in the heavens, mysteriously planned, icy, mechanical, alight, untouching.

In the morning the women returned to the chamber. It may be that experience told them what they would find, for they came with bowls of hot water and with folded cloths. The eldest of the women carried a small knife and a stone, and she hummed an old tune to herself as she crossed the chamber. Light raised beams of dust from the tiny windows. The only sounds were of the women's clogs on the rushes, the cloths being dipped in the water and squeezed out and the barely audible tune, half hummed, half whistled between the teeth and the lower lip, not varying much from the monotone:

'Ble caiff nhad gysgu?
Caiff gysgu yn gwely'r morwynion.'

When they drew the curtains of the bed, they found the novice shaking in terror.

20

Tetty and Geoffrey had decided they must enter the Abbot's house. It was not the first time that Tetty had stood outside, pulling at the bell foolishly while nothing happened, and Geoffrey felt enough concern for the fate of his master not to behave like a polite visitor. The door was not locked, so they went inside.

In such a house it was not easy to find the occupant, though known to be there. Room after room bore evidence of his recent presence: the robe in which he had delivered his sermon lying across a table, papers half-written on, a bowl with food in it (which proved to be, when Tetty looked more closely, some sort of uncooked offal in a strange liquid like vinegar).

They went down corridors, knocking on doors. They left rooms that they found empty by other doors than they had come in by. They went upstairs, and then down again by different staircases. Tetty was clutching a fragment of paper which she had cut out herself with a pair of scissors from the recipe book under instructions from Mrs Ffedderbompau, and on which Mrs Ffedderbompau had written a message to be delivered to the Abbot when she was dead. The message had been sealed with infinite pains—pointlessly, since Tetty could not read. She did not bother to think of what it might contain.

Since Mrs Ffedderbompau's death she had been thinking continually of what Geoffrey had eagerly proposed to her almost as soon as they had met, that she should leave the island with him when Vane's work was done, and that they should marry and live together until they were old people with memories and married children of their own. She had laughed then, and told him tales of boys who were deceived into marrying fairies. And Geoffrey had laughed, too, and they had looked for mushrooms together, he finding none and she knowing as if by magic where they had sprung up overnight. She wondered if all overnight changes were as fragile as these nude pink uncurling creatures, which so shortly blackened and spoiled if not taken up quickly, and knew from the buds of her own body that some were not. Still, fairy or not, particularly not, she felt a yearning to be gathered. And wondered at Geoffrey's ignorance as he pounced with pride on stones, wool tufts, sheep bones, daisie, anything white to the eye at the distance of a house.

She had left the other farm girls talking about what should be done now that Mrs Ffedderbompau was dead. The season constrained them to carry on with harvest; cutting, plucking, garnering. The work would be done. Next season's work would be organised. But for Tetty something had snapped in the life of the farm itself, and now she was ready to leave.

Geoffrey's news that his master had not emerged from the watery foundations of the Abbot's house, and that the channel now appeared to be quite flooded and impassable, had not entirely displeased her.

'Then he must be drowned,' she had said. 'Now we can leave the island, can't we?'

But Geoffrey felt the pull of duty, and was determined to find out if Vane had made his way into the cellars of the Abbot's house and avoided drowning after all. Tetty dismissed the idea as they searched the house for the Abbot:

'If we can't find the Abbot himself, how should we find your master?' she said. 'It must be the Saint's vengeance upon him for tearing up his sacred well.'

'Dear Tetty,' said Geoffrey, with his hand at her cheek. 'Saints don't take revenge. That's why they are saints.'

'Then you are a saint, too, for caring for the man who killed your horse.'

'I don't *care* for him at all,' Geoffrey replied.

'Neither do I,' exclaimed Tetty. 'So when we have given the Abbot the letter we can leave, can't we?'

'I suppose we can.'

'And you can leave the service of such a destroying man.'

'Perhaps I can.'

'Finally, you see,' persisted Tetty, 'he has destroyed himself, in the very waters that should revive him.'

The debt to Vane cancelled by such an argument, they sealed their pact to make a new life together. And as if the house had until that moment of decision been hiding the Abbot away from them so that they should be forced to search in their own minds as well as through its empty rooms until they finally and certainly found what they were looking for, they straight away came upon him in his dissecting chamber.

The Abbot greeted them without rebuke or surprise, and were it not for the absent and distracted air he wore might have seemed almost eager, intruders as they were in such a place, to have them corroborate the discovery he had made.

'Look here,' he said, lifting up the grey arm of the corpse that lay half-covered on the slab in the centre of the chamber. 'Look!'

He took hold of the corpse's fingers, straightening them out one by one.

Tetty did not wish to look much, and Geoffrey could only think, appalled at what they saw, that Vane had been right after all, and that the Abbot was mad and dangerous. How could he as a man of God be found slopping about in an inch of filthy water, his sandals breaking the gouts and ribbons of black blood and skidding on flaps of skin? His hair was awry, and in one hand he held a saw.

'The fingernails have grown,' said the Abbot. 'The waters not only preserve but revive!'

The young pair were abashed in his presence, all they had come for forgotten. When he asked them, it took them a moment to remember. The Abbot took Mrs Ffedderbompau's letter and held it in wonder as he had held the fingers of the corpse.

'She has died, you say?'

Tetty repeated the news: her mistress was now wrapped in a sheet and awaited burial (which in this weather, thought, Geoffrey, had better not be long delayed). The Abbot reflected again upon this information, looking at the letter as though it were a preliminary token of prompt resurrection, a chance error or dropped clause in the legal bond of death, a feather from an angel. When Geoffrey asked him about Vane, it was his turn to look uncomprehending. The man had ceased to behave with the due deference of a guest; why should he continue to be bothered with the duties of a host? If Vane chose to dismantle the skirts of his house and then get stuck, that was his own affair. He had opened the sacred veins of the island which were now quickly wasting their precious power. If he drowned in these waters it was more than he deserved to be simultaneously revived by them.

'He was concerned about the pilgrims,' continued the Abbot. 'Now, by his mining, he has possibly saved them.'

And as if to illustrate this obscure and accidental process of renewal, he worked the block and tackle which hung over the dissecting pit; bringing into view, tethered at the end of the chain, a green foot and its attached leg, raised dripping at an angle like a dancer's.

'Some of these bodies must be very old,' said the Abbot. 'Perhaps they are too old to be brought to life again.'

As an illustration of this rational observation, the foot and shin bone slipped out of the soft sheath of the leg like a piece of over-stewed chicken, and swung gently from the chain.

'But if she were to be brought here quickly,' he added, 'something might be done.'

There was no one to hear these words, for Tetty had run out of the chamber, Geoffrey closely following. He was now convinced that he would get no help from the Abbot. It seemed that it was his master's fate to be ceremoniously dismembered in due course, in the furtherance of some ritual. So be it.

He found Tetty white-faced in the corridor, with one hand steadied against the wall.

'He is stealing the bodies, after all,' she whispered.

'It seems so,' said Geoffrey, 'but they must be carried naturally by the waters down to his house.'

'And is that at all holy?' asked Tetty.

'The Abbot is a troubled man,' replied Geoffrey. 'And that is not holy.'

They could not find the way out of the Abbot's house, and after a while decided to sleep where they were, on the floor, until morning. When they could see better they might the more easily take their bearings, and Geoffrey was sure that by keeping to the outside rooms and noting the position of the sun, they would eventually find the door. They slept badly, in fear of the Abbot, but they saw no more of him.

They had been woken at first light by the screams of the novice which reached them from the distant chamber of his ordeal. Drowsy, they were unsure of what it was they had heard. It was a sound out of nature, at once piercing and furtive, relating only to the lost darkness and only heralding its own indignity.

'That was neither owl nor cock,' said Geoffrey.

Tetty said nothing, but took his hand tightly as if the shocking sound had been the announcement of his own suffering. Using his method, with the added precaution of opening all the doors they passed so that they should not pass them twice, they managed after about quarter of an hour to make their escape.

21

The girls in the last hay field were stooping and tying the fallen swatches of dried grasses and propping the bundles into squat sweet-smelling tents. The fully exposed stubble had now been baked by the sun into a remorseless carpet of spines and quills, which pierced their bare feet as though the cut field had steeled itself against further assault. The work would be done before the morning grew too hot. Then there were dairy tasks, and the preparation of the girls' clothes for the funeral.

Tetty had collected her belongings from the farm and almost no one had seen what she was doing, because the younger girls were all waiting with awe and suppressed excitement for the return of Gweno. She had taken Blodwen aside and told her what she was doing. 'Now Blodwen, don't cry,' she had said, touching the girl's nose. 'You may bring the cows home from now on. And don't forget to turn the cheeses.' Then she joined Geoffrey in the orchard, where they picked a few apples before making their way to the harbour.

'Where are we going?' he asked.

'Anywhere,' said Tetty.

'Anywhere is nowhere,' he replied. 'And how do we know that the boatman will come?'

'You said that he was expected today.'

'Yes, but what if he does not come?'

'We could swim across.'

'Never.'

The haymakers watched them as they passed, with a silence belonging to neither wonder nor envy. Birds above the island wounded the sky with their small rusty strokes of sound, and the high sun in a cloudless sky lit its hills like the limbs of a lazy beast stretching in the warm flood of the sea as though nothing could move it, ever.

The island had seen many arrivals since the days of its first settlement, but it did not let men go willingly. How much easier it is to be a pilgrim of the spirit than to be a pilgrim of the flesh. The one, with nothing to lose and everything to gain; the other with everything to lose. The sublimest caution arises from the discovery and pursuit of the commonplace, for when that proves to be a false haven then all anchorage is lost. But even when true, it is an insecure base for further exploration.

The boatman did not come that day, and Geoffrey and Tetty ate bread in the shade of a gorse bush. They knew that the longer they waited the more they would recognise the power of the dead to keep them from making a new life. At the end of the afternoon the Manciple appeared on the cliff edge a hundred yards away. When he ostentatiously urinated into the sea, they knew that he had seen them; and it seemed that their chances of leaving the island were as slender as his will could make them.

As the sun began to decline, sheep left shade to look for water. The heat was now unfocused and diffused. The cows stood in the hidden reefs of clay beneath the foam of the beach, half-unwilling, half-unable to move, lashing idly at bullying crowds of flies with their tails.

The island prepared for obsequies, but not all the bodies could be found. Vane's last puzzle about the absence of ordained brothers was answered for him by the inquisitive knife, though he was in no position to appreciate this reply. The brain, theoretically projected on to a plane, would be surface enough for crabbed speculation, a grid of prophecies— but the organ was shrivelled and loose, like a waterlogged bladder.

The Abbot was splashing now, the viscosity of the micro-scopically animated well-water gluing the hem of his robe to his ankles as he somnambulated to his library, carrying his letter from Mrs Ffedderbompau. He had taken off his sandals at the first sign of their independent movement against the soles of his feet. He feared what he might find there, feared the process of animation induced by the miraculous spring, feared the active weight and muscle of the words and bindings of his once-still books. It must be the curing of the leather, he argued, that rendered it capable of returning to its former shape. The half-decay of the corpses took them beyond the scope of such metamorphosis. Now, if he were able to have her body tanned!

Some thought of consulting the Egyptian authorities had brought him to the dangerous level of the library, where he had to struggle through the sprouting thicket of the beams, bending aside the sappy branches that sprouted from the panels of the door. Too late? What had happened to all that inscribed wisdom? Was it wasted on the fetid air in the vanishing shape of bellowing and the breath of beasts? Or had the vellum rumination already passed its cud of know-ledge from the ultimate tract? Would he, if he could gain access to the library, merely slither upon a useless excrement of instruction and philosophy?

He stood with his hand upon the knotted bark of the library door in despair as it thudded against his palm with the weight of the huddled herds inside. The living books seemed to have sensed his presence: the bellowing increased as they jostled on the other side of the strained wood, and the ring of hooves on the flooded stone blended with a fresh trumpeting of panic and rebellion. Too late!

Words were indeed more enduring than the body. Mrs Ffedderbompau's letter had fallen from his fingers as he had battled with the foliage, and had lain for a few minutes in the warm well water. Now small shoots of reeds pushed up from the paper, and hair-like roots wriggled to seek the lodging of cracks in the stone. Gall and insect ichor trickled down the fronds, and from the bubbling seal came a sweet stench of wax and a buzzing murmur. The Abbot stooped in sudden love to this miniature landscape which spread like a riverbank by his feet. Shapes were busy in the rushes, crawling up towards the swelling heads of seed. Mrs Ffedderbompau's last words were in his head, like a drowsy charm; and on the edge of his hearing, louder than the stampede of his library, though reduced and distant, rose for an endless moment the purposeful clamour of tiny wings.